River Season

Jim Black

RIVER SEASON

VIKING

VIKING
Published by the Penguin Group
Penguin Putnam Inc., 375 Hudson Street, New York, New York 10014, U.S.A.
Penguin Books Ltd, 80 Strand, London WC2R 0RL, England
Penguin Books Australia Ltd, 250 Camberwell Road, Camberwell,
Victoria 3124, Australia
Penguin Books Canada Ltd, 10 Alcorn Avenue, Toronto, Ontario, Canada M4V 3B2
Penguin Books India (P) Ltd, 11 Community Centre, Panchsheel Park,
New Delhi – 110 017, India
Penguin Books (N.Z.) Ltd, Cnr Rosedale and Airborne Roads, Albany,
Auckland, New Zealand
Penguin Books (South Africa) (Pty) Ltd, 24 Sturdee Avenue,
Rosebank, Johannesburg 2196, South Africa

Penguin Books Ltd, Registered Offices:
Harmondsworth, Middlesex, England

Published in 2003 by Viking Penguin,
a member of Penguin Putnam Inc.

10   9   8   7   6   5   4   3   2   1

Originally published under the title *There's a River Down in Texas*.

PUBLISHER'S NOTE
This is a work of fiction. Names, characters, places, and incidents either
are the product of the author's imagination or are used fictitiously, and any
resemblance to actual persons, living or dead, business establishments,
events, or locales is entirely coincidental.

LIBRARY OF CONGRESS CATALOGING IN PUBLICATION DATA
Black, Jim, date.
River season / Jim Black.
p.   cm.
ISBN 0-670-03227-1
1. Teenage boys—Fiction. 2. African American men—Fiction. 3. Male
friendship—Fiction. 4. Race relations—Fiction. 5. Texas—Fiction. I. Title.
PS3602.L29 R5 2003
813'.6—dc21   2002038003

This book is printed on acid-free paper. ∞

Printed in the United States of America
Set in New Caledonia • Designed by Francesca Belanger

For Loretta Lu

River Season

Prologue

THE LITTLE WICHITA RIVER isn't much of one. Four miles north of Archer City, Texas, where the highway crosses, it's barely twenty feet across and ten feet deep. Usually the bed is dry and cracked, and only after a hard rain does it run at all; then it flows slow and muddy—the water turned ocher by the clay of north-central Texas. Although it drains a small portion of three counties, the river doesn't serve much purpose. The land is flat and mostly barren, and the rocky soil allows little growth other than some mesquites and sparse bluegrass. Some fifteen miles downstream the river empties into Lake Arrowhead, and when it's running good, catfish will leave the lake and swim upriver to feed. This usually attracts a few fishermen, but otherwise, people around here just don't pay the river much mind.

As a boy, though, I spent a lot of time on the banks of that little river. I loved to fish, and even caught a few, but there was another reason. There was something about that river. Sitting on its bank and watching it gave me a good feeling. I could sit there for hours—the steady flow of the water reminding me of things past and those yet to come. The river became my friend. One who would always listen. And like a good friend, the river was dependable. I knew that in time, the water would go down and its banks would be empty; but also that someday it would rain hard again, and the river would return once more.

I was thirteen in the summer of 1966 when I first stood on its banks, and if that summer were a shirt I could wear, that muddy water would be the fabric from which it was made. That was the summer of Sam and Rose and Tick the Dog. The Walking Man. Charles and Gary. And a skinny girl with big brown eyes and flip-flops.

One night that summer the stars fell. And one day I found the Garden of Hearts. And all summer long, I learned about the River Big. I remember wishing that summer would never end, and in a way it hasn't. It changed me forever. An *eternal summer*. And while it began and ended with the river, it also began and ended with Sam.

So shall I. . . .

Part One

EARLY SUMMER

Chapter 1

COOT ONCE SAID that life dealt Sambone a straight flush and then canceled all bets.

All I knew was he was in my spot. My own private fishing spot. I watched him for a while, saw he wasn't leaving, and finally made my way down the bank.

"Having any luck?" I asked.

He looked up, surprised.

"Oh yeah, oh yeah," he said. "Done caught supper. Workin' on breakfast now." He reached down and lifted up a rope stringer with two big catfish on it.

"Dang, those are nice ones," I said. (They were, too.) "What'd you catch them on?"

"Kidney," he said. "Best bait there is. Yessir. You know you can get it for free down at McWhorter's Food Store?"

"No," I said. "I've been using shrimp."

He shook his head in disappointment. "Nope, that won't do. Just won't do, son. Got to be kidney here."

"I've been having a little luck here, too."

"Have I got your spot?" he asked, like he was apologizing.

"No, not really. I've fished here a couple of times, but I never caught any *that* big."

"Well, sit yourself down here, and let's see if you can."

I sat down beside him and started to bait my line.

"Try this here," he said, handing me a piece of his bait.

I placed it on my hook, and just as I was about to throw it out, he stopped me.

"Hold on there!" he said as he caught hold of my line. "Yep, just as I figured."

"What's wrong?" I asked.

"It's that sinker of yours—it ain't near big enough. You got to get a bigger one than that."

"How come?"

"Son, people just don't give this here river enough credit. Current's way too strong for that piddly little thing."

I glanced out at the slow-moving water.

"I know it don't look it on top, but down below, that river's busy. Ain't no way that thing there can get you to the bottom where you need to be. Here, use this." And he handed me a rusty old lug nut. It weighed a ton.

"Will *this* work?" I asked.

"Sure. Those fish don't care what it looks like."

I tied it on and threw it out.

We sat for a while and just fished. I glanced over at him and noticed his eyes were closed. He held his pole in one hand and his line between the thumb and forefinger of the other. He looked to be about sixty years old. His hair was closely cropped and spotted with gray. He had on a tattered pair of khaki pants and worn-out sneakers. He was thin as a rail, and his plaid cotton shirt seemed much too large.

Finally, he opened his eyes.

"My name's Jim Black," I said.

"Samuel Joseph Washington," he replied. "My friends call me Sam, and you can, too."

Just then a raggedy old dog came sliding down the bank and, after coming to a stop, sat down beside him. He cocked his head and looked at me.

"Who's *that?*" I asked.

"This here's Tick the Dog," Sam answered.

"That's a funny name for a dog."

"Only one he'll answer to, and that's the truth. Probably sounds a little classier to him than just plain old Tick," Sam said with a wink.

"What kind of dog is he?"

"Take your pick," he said, smiling. "Whatever you choose, most likely he's got part of that in him. I've always said he's the purest mutt around—oughta be registered."

"Where'd you get him?"

"Found him right up there along the fence thirteen years ago. I's walkin' along and heard somethin' whimperin' down in the brush. When I bent down and looked, all I seen was these ticks. They was all over somethin'. They was all about to bust, they were so big. Then I seen it was a puppy. Couldn't have been very old at all. So I carried him back to the house and lit the end of a hickory stick and burned 'em off, and all the while, he kept lookin' up at me with those sad eyes. And there was somethin' else—*he looked confused*. It was like he was askin', 'Who are you? Why are you doin' this?' It was like he thought that was the way life was supposed to be—nothin' but sufferin'. I'll never forget that look in his eyes. Anyway, I nursed him back to health, and he's been with me ever since. I guess there just ain't nothin' he wouldn't do for me."

I watched Sam lovingly scratch the old dog's head and suspected that, the truth be told, there wasn't anything they wouldn't do for each other.

Chapter 2

THE DOORS TO THE ROYAL THEATER flew open, and as usual, we were the first three out. We turned right and headed down the sidewalk. Past the City Cleaners. Past the City Barber Shop. Past the Lucky Dollar Food Store. Finally, at Bate's Texaco, Gary and I halted beneath the safety of the streetlight.

"I don't give a flip what anybody says—*that* was scary."

"I'll say," Gary answered.

"How would you know? You didn't see half of it."

"Did too."

"Couldn't have. You had your jacket over your head."

"I was watching through the sleeve."

"*Sure* you were."

"I *was!*"

"I think you're *both* pansies," Charles said as he arrived.

"Well, what did *you* think about it?" I asked.

"I thought the blonde's tits weren't bad," he answered as he lit up a Marlboro.

"Was that Bette Davis or Joan Crawford?" Gary asked.

"Janet Leigh," I replied.

"Well, whoever it was, she can scratch my back anytime," Charles said.

"Is that all you ever think about?" I asked.

"What else is there, Bubba?" he answered.

Charles hardly ever called anyone by their real name. He always called me Bubba, and he always called Gary Porky. We, on the other hand, pretty much just called him Charles. He was the best-looking of the group. And while Gary and I mostly wore tennis shoes, he wore penny loafers. (Girls go for style.) We were a thirteen-year-old version of the Odd Couple. Only there were three of us. Above all, we were best friends.

"Okay, whose house are we walking to?" I asked.

"Mine's closest," Gary volunteered.

"Nah, too many dogs down that way. How about yours, Charles?" I asked. Charles had six sisters. At the time, I had a crush on three of them. Besides, his remark about the blonde's tits was still on my mind.

He blew a perfect smoke ring and announced, "Y'all go ahead. I think I'm gonna hang around up here for a while and check out the action."

"*Action?* What kind of action are you going to get? You don't even have a car," I protested.

"Don't need one. Some of the high school girls do."

"*High school* girls? What would a high school girl want with *you?*"

"Yeah, your sideburns aren't even even," Gary added.

"Are *too!*"

"Are *not!*"

"Damn sure are! Besides, at least I've *got* sideburns!"

"Okay, guys!" I interrupted. "Let's not stand here and argue all night. How about we walk to my house and have some Cokes and Chips Ahoys? Then you can spend the night, or I'll get Mom to take you home. What do you think?"

"Sounds good to me," Gary said.

"That'll work," Charles replied. "Besides, it doesn't look like there's much going on tonight anyway."

"Run or walk?" I asked, looking at Gary.

"Run, but not too fast," he responded as he took out his inhaler. He took two quick hits from it and was off.

We set out after him. School had been out for a week now, and our whole summer lay ahead of us. All was right with the world. It was a warm night and smelled of fresh-cut grass and gasoline. Above us, a diamond sky about to burst. Behind us, the worries and cares we shed as we ran. Ahead, the wonder and magic this summer held. Our hearts were pounding— about to burst, it seemed. We ran across our town. Into the night. As if we were trying to catch a train. Or a ghost. Perhaps even life itself.

We ran.

Chapter 3

THE WALKING MAN lived in a tiny house down behind the baseball field and mostly came out at night. He wore a leather motorcycle jacket (collar turned up) and a Houston Astros baseball cap (pulled down low) year-round. And he walked everywhere, always staring at the ground—didn't seem to own a vehicle of any kind. If he had a real name, we didn't know it because folks around town just called him Harley. We three had never seen the Walking Man up close. But we were about to.

Gary was still out in front. Charles and I hung back a ways, knowing we could catch him when we chose to. He had about a thirty-yard lead on us, and it was still over a block to my house. We watched as he turned right sharply at the Garlingtons' and headed up the alley. Then we heard him scream.

We smiled at each other and continued after him. The three of us were all accomplished practical jokers and rarely fell for each other's anymore. We rounded some mesquites, turned right, and stopped in our tracks.

Gary was in a squatting position, fists flailing about and screaming at the top of his lungs. The Walking Man was staring at the ground, pacing back and forth from fence to fence, muttering something I couldn't make out. He looked disoriented. Finally, he turned and started down the alley. He was walking in fast short steps and shaking his head as he went. Gary continued to scream.

Charles grabbed him. "Quit your yelling, he's gone!"

I watched as the Walking Man disappeared from view.

"He's gone, I tell you. You hear me?"

Gary opened his eyes and looked around. He stood up.

"He had me. The Walking Man had me! You guys saved my life."

"What happened?" I asked. "What did he do?"

Gary took out his inhaler and sucked. We waited for him to get his breath.

"It happened so fast. I mean, I just turned the corner, and next thing I knew, he had me."

"What do you mean, he *had* you?"

"He had hold of me. It was horrible."

"Did you get a good look at him?" I wanted to know.

"Sort of. I mean, it was dark, and he had that cap pulled down real low."

"So what did he look like?"

He swallowed hard. "It was horrible," he said.

"*What* was?" Charles was losing his patience.

Gary paused. He stared back down the alley, then at us. He ran a hand across his burr haircut and looked us straight in the eye.

"His tongue," he said, "it was *this* long." He held his hands about a foot apart.

"*What?*" Charles exclaimed.

"His tongue is *huge*—about this long."

"Are you sure?" I asked.

"That or he was eating a foot-long wiener," Gary answered.

"Are you sure he grabbed you?" I asked. "I mean, are you positive you two didn't just run into each other? Heck, he looked just as scared as you."

"No, I'm almost certain he grabbed me. I tell you, I think I was a goner for sure if you two hadn't showed. Think we oughta call the cops?"

"And tell them *what?* That the Walking Man had you and would have licked you for sure if we hadn't shown up?" I said.

Charles laughed. "Yeah, I wish we hadn't gotten here so soon. I'd like to have seen what he was going to do to you with that tongue of his."

"Very funny," Gary said.

"I tell you, it does piss me off that he's out here sneaking around at night," Charles said. "Probably he's a damned old Peeping Tom."

"Well, if he is, he's probably coming to your house some night, with all those sisters you got," Gary said.

"I'd like to catch him peeking in our house. It'd be the *last* house he ever looked in, I'll tell you that."

"Oh yeah, I bet."

"It would, and I guarantee you one thing—he'd need more than just that big old tongue if I got ahold of him."

"It was horrible," Gary said.

"Are you sure you haven't read just one too many *Famous Monsters* magazines?" I asked.

"No, dammit! I haven't," he answered.

"Just kidding," I said. "Besides, you're famous yourself now. You tangled with the Walking Man and lived to tell about it."

"Barely," Gary said, taking one more look down the alley. "Just barely."

Chapter 4

"Back to try again, heh?" Sam said as I started down the bank.

"Yeah, and look what I've got," I answered, proudly holding up a plastic bag of McWhorter's finest giveaway calf kidney. "This oughta last us a while."

"I should say so," Sam replied. "What else you got there?"

"Biggest ones I could find," I answered as I held up a package of my new store-bought lead fishing weights.

Sam smiled big and said, "Son, those poor fish don't stand a chance."

I sat down beside him with Tick the Dog between us. "Can I pet him?" I asked.

"Absolutely," Sam answered. "He's got the same taste in friends I do."

I patted him and scratched behind his ears. He looked up at me and licked my hand. There was no asking *why* in his expression now. Sam had seen to that. I baited my line and threw it out. Then I lay back and held the pole propped against a knee. This was heaven for sure. It was ten in the morning and about seventy degrees. The sky was blue and clear except for a handful of puffy clouds, and there was just a smidgen of a breeze. A perfect day.

I looked over at Sam. He had on the same pants and shoes as the day before, but today he wore a white cotton T-shirt. It, too, seemed too large. He was holding his pole in one hand and petting Tick the Dog with the other.

"You fish every day?" I asked.

"Just about," he said. "Whenever I'm not workin'."

"I figured you were retired."

"I don't reckon that'll ever happen." He smiled.

"How come?"

"Never had a job that paid much. So I guess I'll just work right up to the day I call it quits."

"Where do you work now?"

"Here and there. I sell most of the fish I catch—but this river don't always run, so I can't count on that. And I clean up down at the barbershop after hours. And usually I manage to take in a little down at the shack."

"Where's that?"

"The poker shack," he said. "I can flat play a little cards, if I say so myself."

"I know where that is. My grandparents live just up the road from it. I've walked past it a lot, but usually there's no one there."

"Mostly we play at night."

"I know one thing," I said, "someone there drinks an awful lot. Usually those two barrels out front are plumb full of empty beer cans."

"Yessir, as a matter of fact, most of the participants do like a cold one every now and then. I have noticed that."

"Do you drink?" I asked.

"Not anymore," he said.

"How come?" I questioned.

" 'Cause if I did, three things would happen. First, I wouldn't win as much money. Second, I most likely couldn't find my way home. And third, if I did, my dear Rose would surely make me wish I hadn't." He laughed again.

"Is Rose your wife?"

"That's slicin' it a bit thin," he said. "*Wife* just don't quite get it done. Nope, she's *everything* to me, son. No less. Her given name is Rosella, but to me she'll always be my Rose." He paused. "That woman has pieced and held me together more times than I can remember. She deserves much more than she has, that's for sure."

I watched Sam close, and for a moment it seemed he might cry, but he looked away and I couldn't tell.

"Why'd you ask if I drank?" he asked.

I hesitated and then answered, "I just wondered. My dad used to drink."

"Does he still?"

"No. He died. That's why we moved here from Lubbock. He died in a car wreck."

My own eyes had filled with tears now.

"I don't remember much about him. But I do remember he loved baseball. We used to play catch in the back yard, and he'd always make me practice bunting. I didn't like to, but he said it was a fundamental, and I had to have them all if I was going to amount to anything as a ballplayer. And I remember watching ball games on TV with him."

I stared down at the ground between my legs and felt something touch my hand. Tick the Dog was licking it.

After a moment, Sam spoke. "Do you still like baseball, son?" he asked

I nodded. "I play in a league," I managed to say.

"That so? What position?"

"Center field."

"That's a *fine* position. Yessir."

I smiled but didn't look up.

"You know what? I love baseball, too. Fact is, I used to play a little myself."

"Where at?" I quietly asked.

"Played some in the Negro Leagues a while back. A long while back, I guess you could say."

I looked at him. My eyes were still moist. "That's *pro* ball," I said.

"That's what *we* thought," he said with a smile. "But most folks saw it as somethin' less. They were wrong, though, because we flat out had us some players. Yessir. I know."

"What position did you play?"

"I pitched, son," he said.

"Really?"

"Sure did. And not too badly, I think you could say. Even threw myself a no-hitter once."

"You're kidding!"

"No sir. But that wasn't my best game. The best one was a two-hitter I tossed in a exhibition against the St. Louis Cardinals. Struck out fifteen of them redbirds. And that wasn't the best part."

"What was?" I asked eagerly.

"Well, in the ninth we was leadin' one to nothin', and for some reason I developed a case of the jitters—walked the first three batters."

"What happened then?"

He smiled big. "Struck out the side, includin' Stan the Man with the bases full."

"You struck out *Stan Musial?*"

"Yessir. Twice. Got him in the fifth inning, too."

"Wow, you must have been pretty good."

"I oughta been. I learned from the best. The Satch himself."

"Satchel Paige? No joke?"

"Yep. We's teammates for a while. Even ran together. I still got the glove he signed for me back then. I made him sign it, and told him, 'Someday this is gonna be worth somethin' 'cause you're gonna be great.' And he was."

"You still have it?"

"Absolutely. Would you be interested in seein' it?"

"I sure would."

"Well then, let's mosey up to the house. We might even manage to scare up a couple of ice-cold sodas. Whadda you say?"

"You bet!"

We laid our poles on the ground and put a rock on each to hold them; then we climbed the bank and followed Tick the Dog east along the river.

Chapter 5

SAM AND ROSE'S HOUSE was about a mile from our fishing spot. It once was a bunkhouse for the hired hands of the Muleshoe Ranch back in its heyday, but the ranch was no more, and now it enjoyed more peaceful times as a home.

Rose was outside hanging clothes when we arrived.

"Rose, darlin'," Sam called out, "we have company—mighty important company."

She turned and looked in our direction.

"This here is Mr. Jim Black—a fisherman of the highest order and a scholar of the fine game of baseball."

As thin as Sam was, Rose was equally as large. Very large. She wore a cotton dress full of flowers. And while Sam's face showed his age and the wear of hard times, her own was youthful and almost angelic.

"How do you do, Jim?" she asked.

"I'm fine, ma'am. It's nice to meet you."

"Of course, any friend of Sam's is a friend of mine, and I must tell you, if you like baseball and like to fish, then you're his friend—like it or not. Now, if you gentlemen walked all the way up here just to help me hang these clothes, you're late. So I guess you'll just have to settle for a cold Coke Cola and some of my fresh-baked apple fritters," she said, her eyes squinting as she smiled.

Sam and I grinned at each other.

"Well now, we just might be persuaded at that," Sam kidded.

I was starved. "I guess I could manage that," I added.

"Well, you two wait there in the shade of the porch, and I'll have it right out," she said as she picked up her clothes basket.

"We best do that, son," Sam said. "It don't look it right now, but there could be a mighty big storm right here, right soon, if we don't do as we're told."

I laughed and followed him to the porch. Tick the Dog was there waiting.

In no time, Rose appeared with ice-cold bottled Cokes and a platterful of fresh, hot apple fritters. I'd never tasted anything so good. I ate three, Sam two and a half, and Tick the Dog a half. We had barely finished when Rose appeared again to collect the platter and bottles. She laid a ball and glove in Sam's lap.

"Thank you, darlin'," he said as he handed me the glove.

It was an old Rawlings "Big Daddy," and had been well cared for—that was evident. It had a distinct oily, leathery smell and felt real good when I put it on. Along the front, in big blue letters, was the name SATCH. I looked over at Sam.

"You weren't kidding," I said.

"No, that was the straight scoop. Now, that glove means a lot to me, but there's no reason you can't use it in a game of catch. How 'bout it?"

"What are you going to use?"

Sam laughed and said, "Son, I don't need a glove—these hands of mine are like leather themselves. Don't you worry about me—I'll be just fine."

He stood and walked out into the yard. There wasn't much in the way of a lawn—mostly it was just wild buffalo grass and dirt and stickers. I walked over next to a large mesquite tree and squatted down into a catcher's position.

"All right, show me what you've got," I kidded.

Sam squinted in, raised the ball to his lips (where he kissed it), then rocked back and, with a high leg kick (high for a sixty-year-old) and a big smile, let it go.

It came in with a graceful arc about head high, and just as I reached out to catch it, it suddenly dropped, almost straight down it seemed, and hit the ground and skidded away. I watched it come to a spinning stop next to the clothesline pole. Tick the Dog picked it up and returned it to Sam. He was still smiling.

"What happened?" I asked. I wasn't sure.

"Sun must've been in your eyes. Let's try again."

I got back into position, and once more Sam wound up, kissed the ball, kicked high, and let loose. I followed it closely as it came in, and reached out to snare it. Again, at the last instant, the bottom just fell out, and it dropped under my glove and wound up in nearly the exact same spot by the pole. Tick the Dog was there waiting.

"How come I can't catch it?" I asked, a little bewildered.

"Every pitcher worth his salt has an 'out' pitch. His bread and butter. You just got a couple of looks at mine. I call it my 'call in the boats, the war's over' pitch. Whatcha think of it?"

"What the heck is it? I've never seen one like that before."

"That, son, is the one and only knuckle curveball. Taught to me some years ago by the one and only Satchel Paige. And that's the truth."

"How do you hit it?"

"Most don't. If you looked close, you saw that, besides dropping like a sack of potatoes, it also breaks a little—inside on a right-handed batter and outside on a leftie. Darn near impossible to hit solid. That's a fact."

"Satchel Paige taught you that pitch?"

"Yes, he did. And you know what? He used to say I threw it better than he did. Yessir, we were gonna be somethin', all right. Somethin' special." Sam was staring at the ball as he twirled it in his hand. "We were best of friends back then, and we had this dream that someday we would run onto the field together and listen to the stadium announcer say, 'Ladies and gentlemen, pitching the double-header today for the Washington Senators—Satchel Paige and Samuel Washington.'" He paused, still staring at the ball. "That'd been somethin', all right."

I didn't know what to say. I had the same feeling I'd had listening to Sam talk about Rose back at the river—that he was about to cry. But he didn't. Instead, he looked at me and managed to smile.

"Guess you're wonderin' why that never happened. Well, son, the truth is, I just never managed to handle everything we had to deal with back then—the name-callin', the hate mail, and such. It was always bad, but after we beat the Cardinals, it got worse. It was too much for me."

"What did you do?"

He looked me in the eye. "I drank. I hid. And eventually, I lost everything—except my love for the game itself. I never lost that. Only two things in this whole world I love more are this dog right here and that woman inside that house."

"Maybe it's not too late," I ventured.

Sam eyed me closely. "Just what do you have in mind?"

"You've still got the pitch. That's for sure. Maybe it's not too late to try again."

Sam chuckled and said, "Son, I'm sixty-some-odd years old. I know *I'm* crazy, but I had hope for you. Tell me you're jokin'."

"Why not? What's the problem?"

"Well, runnin', for one. And battin' and fieldin'. Shall I go on?"

"Well, it's a shame there's no place for you to use that pitch, that's all I'm saying."

"Oh, I use it, all right. To impress my friends," he kidded. "Besides, playin' ball again would mean travelin' and bein' away from my Rose and this here dog, and I know for a fact I couldn't manage that for long. Now, what say we agree on that and get back and check them fishin' lines? You may just have a big ol' catfish hooked and don't even know it."

I handed him the glove. As he went inside, I looked around. As far as I knew, Sam and Rose were the only two black people in all of Archer County. They had no phone line, although they did appear to have electricity. The house was in pretty poor shape. Its yellow paint had long since faded, and most of the boards on the porch were weathered and cracked or warped. The tin roof was badly rusted, and in front, one of the windows was boarded up. There was no car, or road, for that matter. It occurred to me that they didn't have much. Not much at all. But there was something they did have. Even at thirteen, I saw it and understood. *They had each other.* And that was enough. That and Tick the Dog.

Chapter 6

GARY'S FULL NAME is Gary Wayne Beesinger, which always sounded like the name of a serial killer to me. AND IN OTHER NEWS—EARLIER TODAY, IN DALLAS, GARY WAYNE BEE-SINGER WAS CONVICTED IN THE SLAYING OF NINETEEN CHEERLEADERS AND SENTENCED TO . . . (see what I mean?) It probably had something to do with the fact he had as many *True Detective* magazines under his bed as he had *Famous Monsters*.

I first laid eyes on Gary as we registered for school in the fourth grade. I was facing a new town, no friends, and a new school. Thankfully, Mom was sitting there with me as I filled out the forms. Suddenly I came to it. *Father's Occupation.* I stared at it blankly and felt my chest tightening. I didn't know what to write. Then she whispered in my ear, "Deceased." Oh my gosh. *Deceased.* She spelled it for me, and I wrote it. No one should have to write "Deceased" next to his dad's occupation. It should go somewhere else. Anywhere. I could barely breathe. At that moment, I looked up from the paper and stared across the room. My eyes came to rest on a kid sitting alone with the exact same look on his face I know I had.

Three years later, Gary still sported a classic blond burr haircut and freckles. And despite still being a little chubby, he managed to provide the most memorable athletic performance I've ever witnessed, a human drama acted out one spring morning on an obscure dirt track in north Texas in the spring of 1966. Our junior high track team was waiting on the bus when Coach

Ryan climbed in and said, "Okay, guys, listen up. Some of the teams can't make it today, so we're going to help out. This means most of you will have an extra event or two." He read them off, then added, "Oh yeah, Beesinger, you're running the hundred-and-ten-yard low hurdles."

The bus exploded with laughter. "All right! Go get 'em, Porky!"

"Sir?"

"You're running the low hurdles. You *can* run, can't you?"

"Yessir. But I've never run any *hurdles*."

"You'll love them."

More laughter.

I knew Gary could run, but he certainly was better suited to what he normally did—which was throw the shotput and discus (although not very far).

"Oh, one other thing," Coach added. "They're giving out ribbons today—the first three finishers in each event."

A cheer went up throughout the bus.

Gary grabbed my arm. "Did you hear that? They're giving out ribbons!"

The drive from Archer City to Holliday is roughly twenty miles, and he didn't say another word the whole way. He just stared out the window.

When we arrived, he and I jogged off by ourselves to loosen up. We found an old hurdle and set it up. I offered what advice I could. "Okay, you're right-handed, so you'll probably want to lead with your left foot. Try that and see." He backed up, took a run, and made it over. He jumped a few more. "You're all set," I said.

When it was time, Charles walked over next to me. "How's he gonna do?" he asked.

"We're fixin' to find out," I said.

The gun went off, and he actually held his own to the first hurdle.

Then it happened. He stuttered his steps at the last instant, jumped awkwardly, and hit the hurdle hard. He crashed to the ground, but got back up and took off again. There was no hesitation in his step at the second hurdle, but he jumped too soon. Another fall. He got back up. Now hopelessly behind, he jumped late at the third and went down hard again. Still, he got back up. The other runners were nearly finished, and he was all but alone on the track. By now he'd caught the crowd's attention.

"Hey, get a load of *this* guy!"

"Hey, shorty, you're supposed to jump *over* those things!"

Reaching the last hurdle, he hadn't cleared a single one and had taken quite a beating. Now, totally exhausted, he paused and then attempted to fling himself over it more like a high jumper. There was a final loud crash, and he went down in a heap.

The finish line was now congested with runners and judges, and most never even noticed as he slowly pulled himself up and started toward them. The few that saw him seemed to stare and wonder where he had come from and what he was doing. Many of the spectators, however, having followed his odyssey, were near tears with laughter. He crossed the finish line and disappeared into the maze of people.

Charles and I looked everywhere for him. Later, we found him in the parking lot, sitting alone in the back of the bus.

"You okay?" I asked as we sat down beside him.

He nodded.

"What happened?"

"I don't know," he said. "I just got to that first hurdle and couldn't remember which foot to lead with. After that, nothing went right."

"Damn, look at you!" Charles exclaimed.

His arms and knees were badly scraped and bleeding. Each one a bright red badge of courage.

"Doesn't that hurt?"

He raised one arm and examined an elbow. He hadn't even noticed. Even his chin was skinned and bleeding.

"I'm sorry," he said. "The last thing I wanted to do was to embarrass you guys and the rest of the team."

"Why didn't you just stop?" Charles asked.

He looked out the window and stared into the distance. His eyes filled with tears.

"Because I kept thinking that if I could just somehow get over that next hurdle, I might still get a ribbon."

We didn't know what to say. For a while, we just sat there without saying anything.

Finally, Charles broke the silence. "Well, if nothing else, it *did* improve your looks. Don't you think so, Bubba?" he said with a wink.

Gary smiled. "It *was* quite a ride out there, that's for sure."

"Yeah," I added, "it was something to behold, all right."

We all laughed. And it was a while before we stopped.

Later that day, I got my ribbon. Charles got two. After the bus was loaded for home, Coach Ryan climbed in and said, "Good job, guys. I'm proud of all of you." He paused for a moment and then said, "Beesinger, get up here!"

Gary shot me a quick, anxious look and slowly made his way to the front. Once there, Coach turned him to face us.

"If any of you ever wonder why I got into coaching, here's the reason, right here," he said, placing his hands on Gary's shoulders. "You know what that Holliday coach said to me while this fellow was making his way down that track? He said, 'Damn, your boys just don't give up, do they?' In all my years of coaching . . . it was my proudest moment."

He ran his hands over Gary's burr and gave him a push. As he made his way back down the aisle, we cheered.

Gary had his ribbon.

Chapter 7

YEARS LATER, in high school, Charles Luig began to exhibit a rare trait. *He could hear a cat walking three blocks away.* That's the truth. He said it was because he had ailurophobia—the fear of cats. Gary and I looked it up in the dictionary, and sure enough, there it was. We always told him it was because of what happened one night that summer.

He had this idea to equip a cat with a homemade parachute and throw it off the water tower. And, of course, he persuaded Gary and me to help him. When we arrived shortly after dark, Charles was there waiting with a parachute fashioned out of one of his mom's sheets, and a black cat (which I quickly decided was not a good omen). Still, everything went fine till about halfway up the tower, when the cat began to get really nervous. By the time we reached the top, it was making a low guttural moaning sound and had pretty much done a job on Charles's junior high football jacket, which he'd cleverly worn for protection. Tossing it off at the top proved to be a bit of a problem. It was screeching and screaming now and hanging on for dear life. Finally, though, Charles managed to wrangle it free and, with a mighty heave, sent it off into cat aviation history. We three watched, enthralled, as the cat plummeted from view, howling to beat all. Then, about halfway down, a curious thing happened. Just before the parachute opened, the cat quit howling. We watched as the chute floated slowly to the ground and landed softly. Then we cheered and hurried down the ladder as fast as we could. When we reached the landing site, the parachute was spread out beautifully over the ground. "Man, can you believe that? That was so cool," Gary was saying.

"It dang sure was," I said.

Charles continued to stare at the sheet. "I don't know," he said solemnly.

"Why? What's wrong?" Gary asked.

Charles reached down and pulled away the sheet. The cat wasn't moving.

"What's he doing?" I asked.

Charles nudged the cat with his foot.

We waited. Nothing.

"He's dead," Charles announced.

"*How?* The chute worked. He landed soft."

"I think he had a heart attack," Charles replied.

"*What?*"

"Remember about halfway down when he stopped making all that noise?"

"I thought that was because the parachute opened and he relaxed."

"Nope. He quit screaming because he had a heart attack. I remember reading somewhere cats have weak hearts. That must've been what happened."

We three stared at the dead cat. "Whose cat is it, anyway?" I asked.

"Nobody's that I know of," he answered.

"He still needs to be buried," Gary said. "And I ain't gonna do it."

"Hell, I guess I will," Charles said. "After all, it *was* my idea."

"I'll do it," I said.

They looked at me.

"Really, I don't mind."

"Suit yourself," Charles said.

I reached down and wrapped the cat in the sheet.

"You sure about this?"

I nodded. "Call me tomorrow, okay?" I heard him say as I walked away. The sheet was so big I felt a little like Rhett Butler carrying Scarlett O'Hara. I wondered if they noticed.

A short while later, I'd walked the three blocks home and was digging a hole in our alley near the garbage cans. I could have buried him anywhere, but decided to do it there as a reminder. When I finished, I decided to unwrap the cat to take one last look at him. Then I saw. *He wasn't dead.*

Barely breathing, but alive. His eyes shut tight, from fear or pain. I stroked him softly on the head. "It's all right," I said. "It's okay." He finally opened them, and I held him up.

The look in his eyes broke my heart.

Why? he was asking. Not unlike the *why* in Tick the Dog's eyes that Sam had talked about. He wanted to know why. And I couldn't tell him. I had no answer for us taking him up that tower—him fighting and begging us not to. And then throwing him off. *He must have been so scared.* I hated the thought of it. I sat down and cradled him in my arms. It was nearly an hour later when I realized he'd died for real. I wrapped him in the sheet and softly placed him in the ground and covered him. Then I sat down beside him and bawled.

It was late when I finally went in. Mom was waiting up. She came into the kitchen, where I was washing up.

"Is everything all right?" she asked.

I nodded.

"I was getting worried. It's pretty late."

"I know," I said. "We lost track of time. Then on the way home I found a dead cat in the alley, and I buried him."

"Does it belong to anyone we know?"

"No. I think it was just an old stray."

"Well, that was nice of you to do that." She touched me on the shoulder. "I think I'll go on to bed."

I nodded good night, and she left.

I was soon crying again, praying she wouldn't hear me. I hated the bottled-up feeling I had inside me. And I had it often. But there was sure no way I could talk about this. How do you tell your mom you threw a cat off the water tower? Still, that's not what was eating at me. What bothered me most was something I had said. *Just a stray*, I'd called it. As though that made it something less. And gave us the right. It didn't. In fact, it made it worse.

Chapter 8

THE RIVER WAS GONE. Its banks empty. I hadn't been to our fishing spot for a week or so, and the river had just plain run its course and petered out. I laid my pole and tackle box on the bank and walked to Sam's.

As I neared the house, I noticed Sam sitting on the porch talking to someone. He saw me coming and stood up.

"Well now, if it ain't my number one catcher and fishin' partner. Come right on up here and have a seat, son. Harold, this here is my new friend I was tellin' you about—Mr. Jim Black."

The visitor stood up and turned around.

It was the Walking Man.

I froze.

He looked at me nervously.

"Harold here's not much of a talker. But he's a great listener—that's what I like about him."

He held out his hand. "Hi, Jim. M-my name's Harold. How g-goes it?"

He didn't remember me. If he did, he didn't show it. I held out my own hand and we shook. "Hello," I said.

His features and voice were soft, his bright green eyes peaceful.

"Did I mention Harold's a fisherman, too?" Sam said. "Yessir. Catches most of his at night, though." He paused and then said, "Sit down, sit down. Well now, this is turnin' out to be one fine day. Just kickin' back on the porch here and takin' it easy with my two good friends—it just can't get much better 'n this. That is, unless we had some of Rose's desserts. I believe I'll go see what I can rustle up for us. I'll just be a minute."

He went inside, and it was a second before I realized the full consequence of the moment. I was alone with the Walking Man. I slowly took my eyes off the screen door and looked at him. He was still staring at the door himself and gently rocking. I thought I could hear him humming.

There was no longer any doubt in my mind that it was the Walking Man, not Gary, who had managed to escape the other night. I couldn't wait to tell him.

"I've seen you walking around town," I ventured. "Mostly at night."

"H-have to," he replied. "I h-hurt at night. Can't s-sleep."

I looked at his cap. "Are you an Astros fan?"

He nodded. "I like to listen on the radio."

"So do I," I said.

He stopped rocking and turned and faced me. "I don't have a great big tongue," he said softly. "And I would never hurt your f-friend."

He knew. I felt terrible. "I know that," I said. "I'm sorry. We were wrong about you. Everyone's wrong."

He leaned back and began rocking again. I watched him for a moment, then Sam returned.

"I don't reckon he's been braggin' to you 'bout his glory days, has he?" he said as he handed each of us a cold Coke and some homemade oatmeal cookies.

"No," I answered. "Sure didn't."

"Naw, he wouldn't," Sam said as he sat down. "But he had 'em. Glory days for sure." I looked over. Harold was still rocking and staring straight ahead, with a hint of a smile.

"Harold here used to race motorcycles. And I ain't talkin' no dirt bikes. No sir. He used to road race. Big time. Drove them Harley-Davidsons."

So that's where he got the nickname.

"And won, too. Ain't that right, Harold?"

He didn't answer.

"Made quite a name for hisself 'fore he was done."

I looked over at Harley, then back at Sam.

"It was a bad spill, son. That's what done it. Happened up in Tulsa. He was eatin' up the straightaway, and the next thing you know, he's down. Just like that. Never knew what caused it. It was the worst kinda spill, too—couldn't get away from his bike. It was like it had a mind of its own. Tangled with the durn thing for a quarter mile. I tell you, it's a flat miracle he's sittin' here today."

Harley's smile was gone. He bit into his cookie.

Sam looked over at me and winked. "Thought that might shed a little light on things for you," he said.

I nodded.

"Well, I said it once, and I'll say it again. This is one fine day."

I agreed.

Chapter 9

WE SAT one hundred and fifty feet above Archer, suspended in time and space; the present and future beneath us, transfixed and earthbound, and the past above us, reflected in ancient starlight. Below, our town moved in slow motion, dreamlike, without us. This was our most private and favorite spot. Here, conversations ran the scale and ranged from pondering life's mysteries (me talking) to favorite pizza toppings and maniac killers (Gary talking) to lingerie, the female anatomy, and such (Charles talking.)

Yes, the water tower was our friend, our haven, our escape. Occasionally, we would simply climb up, attach and light two emergency automobile flares, and disappear. From a distance, the tower resembled a colossal robot with bright red glowing eyes looking out over Archer. Tonight, as we often did, we simply sat, feet dangling, cool breeze in our faces, at each other's sides.

"Are you sure his tongue isn't just a *little* big?" Gary asked again.

"I'm sure," I said.

"And he really is an okay guy?"

I nodded.

"Ain't that somethin'?" Charles was saying. "All this time we've been afraid of someone who probably wouldn't hurt a flea. And you're right—I'll bet he was scared shitless when he ran straight into Porky that night."

"I don't know, I sure thought I was a goner."

"I think you guys should meet him," I said.

"No thanks," Gary said. "I already have, remember? And once is enough—I don't care how he looks in the daylight."

"Nope, me neither. Maybe he used to be a normal guy, but he's sure weird now. Besides, why are you hanging around him?"

"I'm not. I just met him that once."

"And what about Sam?"

"He's a nice guy, and I like fishing with him—that's it."

"Well, do what you have to do."

"You guys won't hold it against me, will you?" I asked.

"Yeah, but we'll get over it," Charles kidded. "Just don't expect me to show up at any of y'all's tea parties."

"Me neither," Gary said. "The Walking Man still gives me goose bumps."

Looking back, I know now that I had the two best friends a guy could ever hope for. And I've often wondered what it was that drew us together. I have an idea that part of it was a common thread we shared—our fathers all drank. And now were gone. Like me, Charles lost his in a car wreck—early one morning right out there at the river bridge near where Sam and I fished. Still, we always thought Gary had it the hardest. His dad just up and left. We never talked about it much. I wish now we had. And something else—I believe there was a reason we were drawn to that old water tower. That perhaps we all were needing something to hold on to, and the water tower provided that. It was strong and sturdy, and it wasn't going anywhere anytime soon.

Chapter 10

AT JOE'S DRIVE-IN you could get a large, greasy cheeseburger, french fries, a large cherry, vanilla, or chocolate Coke, and play the pinball or bowling machine, all for less than a dollar.

One night, Gary and I were hard at work trying to break the world record on the Miss Lots-O-Luck pinball machine. Miss Lots-O-Luck wore a skimpy western outfit and occasionally her two badges would light up. (We loved to watch her badges.)

Outside was one heck of a thunderstorm. We had beat it to Joe's and were warm and dry, but the same couldn't be said for half the people there, who were soaking wet. Joe was listening to the radio, switching channels, concerned about the weather. And while it was true we were in a tornado watch, we weren't too concerned because the bad stuff always hit Throckmorton and Baylor Counties first. Just then, Joe announced to the crowd, "Tornado warning for Baylor County! Got one on the ground just east of Seymour!" Gary and I looked at each other. I think he liked thunderstorms as much as I did, and the idea of a tornado was exciting just as long as it didn't get *too* close. Besides, everyone knows it has to stop raining before you can have a tornado, and outside it was really pouring.

Just then, Charles burst in the door, soaking wet, yelling, *"Twister! Twister, everybody!"*

You should have seen those folks scramble. They were running over each other. Some even ran outside. We didn't move. Instead, we watched Charles shake off the rain and wink.

Alvin Holcomb was the first back in. "Dammit, Luig! I

ought to have known better than to listen to you. *Now* look at me." He was soaked.

"Where's everybody else?" Joe asked.

"Hell, they split!" Alvin said, grabbing a handful of napkins to dry off with. "Went every which way. Thought the funnel had 'em for sure." The three of us were dying laughing.

Joe walked over. "Now, men," he said, "fun's fun, but I just lost some business."

"Okay, Joe," Charles was saying. "I'm sorry. But you have to admit, it *was* funny. I'll bet Gilbert ain't moved that fast in thirty years. He's probably halfway to Olney by now."

Joe smiled. "You just better hope he keeps on going and doesn't come back. Now, how about something to eat?"

"Believe I will at that," Charles said. "Is your hamburger steak fresh, or green as usual?"

"Green."

"I wouldn't have it any other way."

Joe smiled and went back to his grill and radio.

Gary and I finished our game (about 100,000 points shy of the record), and we all sat down in our booth. Just then thunder cracked, and the diner shook. It was coming a flood outside, and I was glad. The river hadn't run in a while. At this very moment, its banks were filling and the river was coming to life.

Shortly, Joe brought Charles's food, and we watched him eat it. Gary went over to the jukebox. After a moment, he returned and some guy began singing about a rainy night in Georgia. It wasn't long before he finished and Charles said, "All right, you guys ready?"

"What do you mean?" I asked.

He held up car keys.

"Whose are those?"

"My sister's," he said.

"You mean Raylette loaned you her car?"

"Well, sort of," he answered. "What she doesn't know won't hurt her."

"She'll kill you," I said. "She'll kill us all."

"You want to go or not?"

"Absolutely! How 'bout you, Gary?"

"We're outta here!" he said.

We started for the door. "Thanks, Joe," we all said.

"You boys come back soon," he replied. "And be careful of that weather out there."

The rain had let up a little; still, we got plenty wet running to the car, a '56 Chevy Belair. It was a great car to have in a thunderstorm. The Belair's windshield wipers operated by vacuum, and whenever you accelerated hard, they just froze until you let up on the gas. And Charles was *always* accelerating.

"Where are we going?" I asked, once inside.

"I thought we'd go to Wichita and cruise Kemp," Charles answered.

"*Wichita?* You don't even have your license! What if you get stopped?"

"Then I'll probably get a ticket, and you guys will help me pay."

"What's on Kemp Street?" Gary asked.

"Chicks," Charles answered.

"Oh yeah, I can see it now—it'll just be lined up solid with good-looking thirteen-year-old girls standing in the pouring rain," I said as Gary nearly died laughing.

"Well, it might be a little slow at that," Charles conceded. "So I guess I'll just have to dust y'all's britches at bowling instead."

"Yeah, tonight's Red Pin bowling over at Spudder Lanes!"

Gary said. "Get a strike with a red headpin, and you win a free game!"

"Well, all I can say is they better watch out or we'll clean house," Charles stated.

We all laughed and kidded as we headed toward Wichita Falls. Just to be safe, we took the long way and stayed mostly on deserted country dirt roads. We weren't quite halfway there when, just like that, it suddenly stopped raining.

"Dang, ain't *that* weird?" I remember saying.

"Guys, I don't like the looks of this," Charles said as he slowed down. We were looking out the windows, but it was pitch-dark, and we couldn't see much. He pulled over and stopped. We all climbed out.

There was no rain and no wind. I'd never seen it so still. Then a lightning flash revealed angry, swirling clouds above us.

"Tornado!" Gary screamed.

"Where?"

"Over there!" he yelled, pointing west.

It was dark. I couldn't see a thing. *"Where?"* I asked again.

A huge bolt of lightning lit up the night, and there it was. Hanging from the sky, not quite on the ground. And white as snow.

"Come on! Let's go!" Charles yelled, and in we jumped and took off. Toward Wichita. "Shouldn't we turn around?" I asked, trying to sound calm.

"Nah, let's get a good look at that sucker—we may never see one again!"

I watched, face pressed against the glass, and waited for the lightning. Finally, it came. The funnel looked to be on the ground now, still to our left about a mile and slightly ahead of us. Charles sped up. I waited for another look.

The lightning struck again and confirmed what I'd sus-pected before—it was moving northeast, and we were headed north. We were going to meet. "Stop the car, Charles! We're headed right for it!"

"We can beat it," he said.

"I don't think so. I think we'd better stop!"

Gary turned the radio on. KTRN had interrupted with a weather update. *"We're getting reports of a wall cloud some-where southwest of Wichita Falls in the Lake Kickapoo area. If you are in the vicinity, take shelter immediately."*

"You hear that? *That's us!* STOP THE DANG CAR!"

It was a couple of moments before another flash lit up the night, and what I saw almost stopped my heart. It was practi-cally on top of us. "Oh shit!" Charles shouted. I was thinking whoever first said tornadoes sound like freight trains knew what they were talking about. The car lurched hard and left the road. We were suspended in midair just feet above the ground. I ex-pected to see a cow fly past. Or a telephone post. We turned and looked at each other. Then suddenly we hit down hard, swerved, and skidded to a stop. And just as quickly as it had started, the wind died, and with it that sound. The funnel re-ceded into the clouds and was gone.

Our car sat in the middle of the road facing the wrong way. For a moment, none of us spoke. Finally Gary did. "I don't know about you guys, but *I've* got to go to the bathroom!"

We all jumped out and stood peeing into the bar ditch. It began to rain. We hurried to finish, and Gary and I jumped back in the car. Charles conducted a brief vehicle inspection and joined us. It was raining hard now, and I was glad because I knew there would be no tornadoes if it was. The wind was still blowing, but it was just a straight wind.

"It almost got us," Gary announced as Charles turned around.

"It's not us I was worried about," Charles replied. "If it'd torn up this car, we'd been goners for sure. Even that twister ain't no match for Raylette when she's mad."

"Wait a minute," Gary was saying. (He beat me to it.) "What's this *we* business?"

"*We,* as in the *three* of us. As in—she'd have whipped all three of our butts, I guarantee you." We laughed again as he accelerated and headed north. "Let's see, I believe we were going bowling," he said, smiling.

Chapter 11

SPUDDER LANES WAS OLD AS THE HILLS but still a fun place. The snack bar was good, the pinball machines were fair, and the girls behind the counter were always cute. Tonight was no exception. Charles seized the opportunity to tease the redhead behind the counter.

"What size shoes?" she asked.

"One sax an one tharteen ana haf," he deadpanned.

"Excuse me?" she asked, a little embarrassed.

"One sax an one tharteen ana haf," he repeated.

"One six and one thirteen and a half?" she asked.

He nodded. She looked over at us. We stood tight-lipped. She reached under the counter and handed him the shoes. He looked at them and said, " 'Scuse mae, but deeze are fore de wrong feet." He stuck out his lower lip in a pronounced pout.

I bit mine to keep from laughing.

She was confused and clearly shaken. Gary came to her aid. "What he said, miss, is you have the six on the left and the thirteen and a half on the right. He needs the six on the right and the thirteen and a half on the left. That's all."

She stared at Gary for a moment. I had to turn and watch the bowlers. She reached back under the counter, switched the shoes, and handed them to Charles. He smiled big and nodded.

Then he asked, "Stockings?"

She looked at Gary. "He needs socks," he said.

"He doesn't have any?" she asked.

"Yeah. But they're wool, and they itch his feet when they sweat."

I had to walk away.

Behind me, I heard her apologize for not having any.

After they had finished and left, I walked over and paid for mine. Then I joined them.

"You guys oughta be ashamed."

"We know," Gary replied. Charles just smiled, getting ready to bowl.

"Aren't you going to wear the shoes?" I asked.

"Are you kidding?"

"The sign says no street shoes allowed. What are you going to do, bowl in your socks?"

"Yep."

And he did, until I happened to look up and see the girl from the counter walking in our direction.

"Here she comes!" I warned.

Charles quickly sat down and put his bowling shoes on, the best he could. Then he went to the ball rack.

"How's he doing?" she asked.

We couldn't tell if she was serious or on to him.

"Pretty good tonight," Gary answered. "He even knocked one down in the last frame."

She smiled but didn't move.

With all eyes on him, Charles concentrated on the pins, took five awkward steps, released the ball, and went down hard face first, shoes flying everywhere.

Gary and I almost fell out of our chairs. We were laughing hysterically. But the girl wasn't. "Oh my gosh! Is he all right? Is he hurt?"

Charles had rolled over on his back and was lying motionless, spread-eagled.

"Yeah. He's all right."

"Are you sure he doesn't need help?" she asked anxiously.

"Oh, he needs help, all right," I said.

Gary laughed. She looked at him, then at me. Then she took one last look at Charles and turned and walked away plenty mad.

He popped up, gathered up the shoes, and hurried back to where we were. People all around us were staring, but he didn't care. He sat down.

"Damn, guys. I thought she'd never leave."

"Well, I have to say that was one of your better falls. It sure looked real," Gary said.

"Hell, it *was*. Look what I was wearing!" He dropped the shoes on the floor. "I don't care how cute she is, she's not worth this." He lifted up two bloody elbows.

He bowled the rest of the night in his penny loafers.

Our bowling wasn't too spectacular that night. We each won a game, but no one got a strike with a red headpin or with the redheaded counter girl. We left.

We stopped at Burger Chef before leaving town and loaded up on fifteen-cent hamburgers, fries, and apple pies. Then we made one quick pass down a deserted Kemp Street and headed home. We were brave now and took the main highway. It rained all the way. As we crossed the river bridge, I tried to see how far up the river was, but it was too dark. At the red light, Charles turned right toward Gary's.

"What's that?" Gary asked.

"Where?"

"There on the corner. Some idiot just standing in the rain."

As we got closer, we saw.

It was Harley.

"It's the Walking Man!" Gary exclaimed.

"Listen, he may be an okay guy, but he's still a nut. What the hell's he doing out here in this weather?" Charles said to me.

It was pouring, and he was soaked. He was standing on the corner, and after we passed, he started across the street.

"Turn around," I said.

"Do *what?*"

"Let's go back and give him a ride."

"You've got to be kidding."

"I'm not. *Please.*"

"You serious?"

"Yeah, I am," I said. "Please, let's give him a ride."

"No way, José!" Gary exclaimed. "You're not putting him back here with me!"

Charles looked at me for a moment square in the eyes. Then he shook his head and wheeled the car around.

"Oh shit!" Gary said, scooting over as far as he could against his door.

When we reached him, I rolled down my window. He stopped and stared at the ground.

"You need a ride?" I asked.

He didn't answer. The rain was beginning to pour into the car window.

"Harold, it's Jim Black. I met you at Sam's a while back."

Still he didn't look up.

"Listen, we'd be glad to give you a ride, seein' as how it's raining and all."

He hesitated. I was getting soaked. And then he nodded.

I reached back and opened the passenger door on his side. Gary tightened his grip on his own door handle. Harley stepped in.

Charles turned to face him.

"This here's Charles Luig and Gary Beesinger," I said. "Guys, this is Harold."

Harley nodded but didn't look up. He sat with his hands folded in his lap. Gary and Charles each said hi and looked him over. Then Charles turned around and we were off.

"You live near the baseball field, don't you?" I asked.

He nodded.

We all knew where he lived. We rode the rest of the way in silence. I couldn't think of anything else to say. Before long, we were there. Charles pulled into the muddy driveway. Harley sat for a moment, then climbed out and softly closed the door. He started to head to the house, but stopped next to my window, staring at the ground. I rolled the window down.

He bent down and looked inside at each of us, one at a time. The rain was pouring off his cap and jacket, and the dash light reflected off his wet face. "Thanks, guys," he said. And then he turned and walked away. We watched him go inside and waited for a light to come on, but none did. We headed home in silence.

It was years before we told anyone about our encounter with the tornado. By then no one believed us. But as much as we wanted to back then, we couldn't. Charles's sisters and mom simply would have killed him. We would never have seen Gary again—he would have been grounded for life for sure. I don't think I would have been skinned alive, but my mom would not have been happy, either. So we kept quiet.

We kept quiet about Harley, too. We didn't even want to think about what Raylette would do if she knew the Walking Man had been riding in her car, and we weren't sure we could make her understand.

Chapter 12

THE CITY BARBER SHOP was a popular place with us. The proprietor, Frank Coot, preferred to be called by his last name. He always wore a clean, heavily starched white long-sleeved shirt and dress slacks, and looked as though *he'd* just gotten a haircut and shave himself. And he always kept a few *Playboy* magazines on hand for the patrons. He was a nice man, and he was funny—should have been a stand-up comic. On top of that, I loved the way the barbershop smelled. All the powder and tonic.

I needed a haircut and looked forward to going. As I stepped inside, I noticed some of the regulars. Hank White and Johnny Sims were playing checkers. And Billy Conklin was admiring the Playmate of the Month.

"Hi there, young-un," Coot said (he always called me that) as I walked in. "Have a seat if I don't mind so myself."

I did. He threw the cape around me and began fastening it in the back.

"I don't guess you've gone and gotten yourself rich or married since I saw you last, have you?"

"No sir," I answered.

"Well, that's a shame. At least the not gettin' rich part. What do you think, Hank?"

"You're disturbin' my concentration," he said, studying his next move.

Coot smiled and said, "What'll it be today, young-un? Mohawk or bouffant?"

"Flattop," I answered. "And this time could you try and get it straight on top? Last time I had to walk with my head tilted to one side for two weeks," I kidded.

He walked around to the front of the chair and peered at me over his glasses. "Did you ever stop to consider that maybe your head ain't exactly flat? Or perhaps the ground you were standing on wasn't level?"

"No sir, I didn't give that much consideration. But I will."

"Well, if it ain't the nigger lover himself," Billy spouted. Evidently, he'd finished his magazine and had just now noticed I'd come in. I wished he hadn't. Billy was a few years older than me and one grade below me in school. And a royal pain in the ass.

I understand you're pretty tight with old Sambone and the Walking Retard—least that's what everybody says."

The others weren't paying him any mind.

"So which one's best? Or do the three of you do it together?"

Finally, Coot spoke. "Son, you're bothering my customer. So either put your nose back in that magazine or put a lid on it."

"I ain't botherin' nobody, am I?" he said, looking at me.

Coot walked around to the front of the chair and with scissors in hand said, "You're botherin' *me*. Now for the last time, *cool* it."

Billy started to speak, but didn't. Instead, he frowned and grabbed a magazine. A minute later, he was totally engrossed in another fold-out.

"Nothin' wrong with that boy a good old fashioned asswhuppin' wouldn't take care of," he whispered.

"I know," I answered.

"However, he *is* a mite bigger than you. That does pose a slight problem, I guess."

He was a *lot* bigger than me.

"Course, there's an answer for that, too," he said. "It's called a two-by-four."

I laughed and said, "I'll remember that."

"And something else, if you don't mind me saying. That boy there probably ain't the only person in this town that feels like he does. He's young and stupid, but a lot of us grew up that way and are still pretty old-fashioned. As for me, I figure I don't like folks gettin' into my business, so I try to make it a point not to get into theirs. And I reckon your friends are your business. Speaking of which . . ."

Just then, Gary walked in.

"Keystone Kop Number Two," Coot exclaimed. "Number Three isn't coming, too, is he?"

"Charles? Nope, he's in Wichita," Gary answered.

"Thank goodness. I don't feel up to tangling with the three of you today."

"You won't have to. Just me and him," Gary said. "Do you have any butch wax?"

"Laddie, in case you haven't noticed, this here establishment is a barbershop. *Of course* I have butch wax. The question is, do you have any money?"

"Sure do."

"Then most likely we can do business. I guess you want a haircut, too?"

"Yep. And this time—"

"I don't want to hear it," Coot interrupted. "You always get a burr haircut, if I remember right. And a burr is a burr is a burr. Period."

"Yeah, but this time can you get my sideburns even?"

"Son, when you get yourself some sideburns, I promise to get them even. But right now, you don't have any, never had any, and probably never will have any. Okay?"

"Yeah, I guess."

"You can have mine if you want," Johnny deadpanned without ever looking up.

"No thank you," Gary said. "I'll just wait."

"Suit yourself," he replied.

"Well, that oughta hold you for a while." Coot removed the cape and brushed my front and back. "If you're meetin' a lady friend, then I'll put some of this on you so you'll smell good. If not, I'm not gonna waste it."

"Naw, save it," I said. "I'm going fishing." I stood up and didn't bother to look in the mirror at my hair. I was afraid Coot might say something. "I'll wait on you if you want to go," I told Gary.

"I can't. Benny's taking us to Olney to eat. Tonight's all-you-can-eat catfish at the No-D-Lay."

"Okay. Well, I'll see you later. Thanks, Mr. Coot."

"Young-un, don't call me mister. My daddy's still alive, and even he don't like bein' called that."

"Sorry. I forgot. Well, I'm outta here."

" 'Bye, young-un."

As I walked out, Billy never even looked up from his magazine. And that didn't hurt my feelings at all.

Chapter 13

IT HAD BEEN A WHILE since I'd been to the river. Charles and I had been busy mowing yards, and until the recent hard rain, there hadn't been a river to fish in. I planned on doing more now, especially since I no longer had to walk or hitch a ride. Today, I parked my new (used, but new to me) Cushman Husky scooter and admired it for a moment. (I had paid fifty grass-mowing dollars for it.) Like all Huskies, it was a two-speed with a slip clutch (great for peeling out) and loud. I loved it. Except for the kick starter. If you didn't watch it close, it would hang up enough that you had to put all your weight on it—then it would give all of a sudden and really hurt your foot. As a result of just such an experience earlier in the day, I was limping slightly as I grabbed my pole and gear and headed for our fishing spot.

I expected the river to be up, and it was. Not only that, it was almost out of its banks. Our usual spot was underwater. Still, Sam and Tick the Dog were there, just above it on higher ground. As I walked over, he smiled.

"Son, if we can't catch fish today, we have no business callin' ourselves fishermen. This here's prime fishin' conditions, simple as that."

I went over next to him and sat down. He noticed I was moving a little gingerly.

"Got a burr in your shoe?" he asked.

"Nope. Me and that scooter had a little battle this morning, and the scooter won."

"There's no mistakin' the sound of a Cushman. Yours an Eagle or Husky?"

"Husky," I said, somewhat surprised.

"Kick starter getcha?"

"Yeah. How did you know?"

"That ain't uncommon with them Huskies. Neither is burnin' your leg on the exhaust pipe. You done that yet?"

"Matter of fact, I have," I answered. "What else can I look forward to?"

"Actually, those are fine machines. I had a Husky once—couldn't afford no car—but Rose made me get rid of it. Said I was gettin' too old. Now, how do you like that?"

I tried to picture Sam on a Cushman.

"But that was all right. Truth is, I was gettin' tired of havin' a sore foot and burnt leg anyway." And we laughed.

I baited my line and cast it out. "Have you caught any yet?"

"No sir. Just got here myself. But it shouldn't be long."

And it wasn't. A second later, he pulled hard on his pole and stood up. He looked puzzled. He was fiddling with his reel and said, "Son, I'm either hung on a log or I got hold of Mr. Bigfish himself." I stood and watched, excited. He continued to battle for several minutes, then managed to get him near the bank. I grabbed Sam's line and followed it to the water. "Careful, now," he said.

I turned to ask why when I felt the line jerk hard. When I looked back down, I jumped two feet in the air and turned loose of the line. Sam had caught the biggest turtle I'd ever seen. Its shell must have been two feet across, and its head was the size of a big potato. It had large, hornlike fins on top of its shell.

"You might wanna come on back up here," Sam was saying. "That's a snappin' turtle. You best stay clear of him."

"Are they mean?" I asked.

"Mean as all get-out and dangerous to boot. I swear, I never knowed one to get that big before."

We watched the turtle for a moment. He was half in and half out of the water. Sam was holding tight on the line so he couldn't get back in. His lips were full of fishhooks, and he was snapping at the air.

"Come take my pole," Sam said. "Just hold tight so he can't go anywhere. I'll be right back."

The turtle and I stared at each other until Sam got back. He was holding a mesquite log about four inches thick and three feet long. I watched as he carefully made his way near the turtle and held the wood out to him. In the wink of an eye, the turtle lurched out and bit the log—almost in half, it seemed. And he wouldn't turn it loose. Sam still had hold of one end and began dragging it up the bank. After he'd done so, he turned loose of the wood. The turtle stood there, log in mouth, shaking his head from side to side, all the while, looking at us. Tick the Dog was also keeping his distance. He never once barked or growled, but rather looked a little bewildered. Obviously, he'd never seen one this big, either.

Sam took out his knife and cut the line. "That feller can add my hook to his collection as far as I'm concerned."

"When's he gonna turn loose of that log?" I asked.

"When he's good and ready," Sam answered. "And that may be a while, as ticked off as he appears. He ain't likin' no part of this, that's for sure."

"What are you going to do with him?" I asked.

"Nothin'. Other than keep a good eye on him so he don't come too close."

"Will he?"

"Most likely not. Probably he'll just sit there and blow off steam for a while, then head back into the river."

"You're not going to kill him?"

"No, son, I'm not. Do you want to kill him?"

I thought for a moment. "No, I guess not."

"Then let's get back to fishin'. We're wastin' good time."

"We're just gonna turn our backs on him?" I asked, more than a little anxious.

"Tick the Dog'll keep a lookout for us. He'll let us know if there's any reason for concern."

We went back to fishing, and I trusted Tick the Dog, but occasionally, I did sneak a peek over my shoulder just to be sure.

"Feller lost his hand in the river, right here, several years ago," Sam was saying. "I always thought it mighta been a snapper. Now I'm sure it was."

"What happened?" I asked.

"He and his buddies were grapplin' one day—"

"What's that?" I wanted to know.

"That's how you catch fish when the river is too low. You wade in and walk along till you find a deep ol' hole, and you just reach down and feel around for any big ol' catfish that mighta been left behind. Sometimes you'll find one holed up there waitin' for the river to rise enough so he can swim out. Anyway, you just reach in there and grab 'em by the mouth or gills. They generally won't put up much of a fight 'cause they're tired and the water's old and stale."

"You're kidding, right?"

"Nope, that there's grapplin'."

"Have you ever done it?" I asked.

He looked at me. "Son, Rose has accused me at times of bein' not too levelheaded, but I can assure you I'm not fool enough to go reachin' down in that muddy water where I can't see," he said with a grin.

"So what happened to this guy?"

"Well, they say he reached down out there somewhere and felt a little tug—that's all. Anyway, when he raised his arm, his hand was gone at the wrist. Well, he started screamin' and passed plumb out right there in the river. Lucky for him, his buddies heard him and pulled him out. One of 'em took some baling wire off the fence up there and wrapped it around his wrist, and they took him to the hospital in town. Never did find his hand."

"Is he still around?"

"Nope. In a way, he died from losing that hand, but it was a whole year later. After it happened, he got real depressed and just went downhill. Lost his job and wouldn't take care of hisself—much less his family. So his wife up and left him and took their son. And he got worse after that. Then one night he drove out to the railroad tracks, laid down next to 'em, placed his good hand on the rail, and waited for the Burlington Northern. Sure enough, it came and went and took his good hand with it. They found him the next mornin' in his pickup over by the hospital. Looked like he tried to drive hisself there but didn't make it. Bled to death 'fore he got there." He paused. "Hard to figure, that's for sure."

I eyed Sam closely. "You being straight with me?" I asked.

"As the crow fly," he said. "And I'll tell you somethin' else. You most likely know his boy. His mama ain't around here no more, but he is. She left him to live with his granny."

"Who is it?" I asked.

"Boy's name is Billy Conklin."

Chapter 14

BILLY CONKLIN may have had a tough go of it in his life, but he was still a jerk. So his dad wasn't around, and his mom left him to live with his grandmother, and so his life was basically screwed up—there was nothing I could do about it. If I could, I would. But there wasn't. The fact remained that, for reasons good or bad, Billy Conklin was a prick.

I thought about this as I sat alone in our usual spot about halfway up the bank. The river was back to normal and the turtle was nowhere to be seen. It had been a few days since Sam had caught it, but when we left that day, he was still standing there waving that stump. Anyway, he wasn't there now, and I liked that fine. Sam wasn't there, either, but it was pretty late, and he had probably been there and gone.

I had done a lot of thinking lately and reached a conclusion of sorts. My feelings over the cat prompted it. This is what I decided: The word *why* is not the bear I once thought it was. Handled properly, it doesn't have to rip your heart out. It will only hurt you if you let it. It's okay to ask why. It's safe to ask why. *If you're careful*.

Why did we throw that poor cat off the water tower?

Why did Harley crash one day, leaving him the way he was?

Why did my dad die?

There were answers to these questions. Basic, straightforward answers.

On a certain level.

We threw the cat off because we didn't stop to think about what might go wrong. And because he was a stray.

Harley's accident occurred because something on his motorcycle broke or because of the carelessness of one of the other drivers. Perhaps even himself.

My dad died because he was drunk and attempting to drive. His judgment, reflexes, and possibly his vision were impaired at the time. And while it's true he had driven that same route many times before while intoxicated—that one time he couldn't. He turned the wrong way down a one-way street and, to avoid hitting oncoming vehicles, veered off the roadway and crashed into a concrete embankment, crushing his chest on the steering wheel. He died soon after, and lives were changed forever.

These were all answers I could accept. It is safe to ask why. That is not the problem. The trouble starts when you try to find the *reason* things happen. That can be overwhelming. If you're not careful, it will eat you up alive.

Did the cat die for a reason? Did Harley's accident happen for a reason? If so, what purpose could possibly have been served? And what about my dad? Or was it just pure chance? Perhaps bad luck.

The search for *reason* can be cruel and lacking in pity, and is best left alone. For, given half a chance, it'll ruin you.

The sun was going down, and the wind was still. Before me, the slow, muddy water slid silently past, carrying with it twigs, insects, and countless other things both dead and alive. In the distance, a coyote howled. Then another. A handful of stars appeared in the eastern sky. It was time to go. I gathered my stuff and walked to my Husky. Once there, I tied my things to the passenger seat and tried the infamous kick starter. It started on the first attempt. I climbed aboard, laid my pole across the handlebars, and sat there for a moment, letting the engine warm.

I looked down at the river beneath the bridge. This was where Charles's dad had died. *This very spot*. Why had it happened? He had fallen asleep at the wheel on his way home early one morning. That was understood. But for what reason? What purpose? I looked away and didn't pursue it.

An eighteen-wheeler roared past and honked. I waved. I turned and looked to the north and saw the glow from the lights of Wichita. In the west, the last shimmering rays faded from the sun. To the east, darkness was gathering up the river. I pulled up onto the highway and headed south. Toward home.

"You live, you die, that's it," I heard someone say once. The perfect solution. No use in wondering. No sense in asking. It doesn't matter. *Perhaps*. But that's a tough idea to swallow at thirteen. Darn near impossible. At thirteen, things matter. A lot.

I topped the hill at Muleshoe Ranch and saw the lights of Archer. As I got closer, I could see the water tower. Suddenly two red lights began to glow brightly near the top. Two fiery eyes. I smiled and sped up. I was alone on the highway. Alone on the landscape. Alone beneath a diamond sky. And like a leaf on the river, I was headed for my destination.

Whatever that might be.

Part Two

SUMMERTIME

Chapter 15

SUMMARY: Summer was in full swing, and I was settling into a routine. When I didn't have ball practice, most of my days were spent mowing yards with Charles. Most nights I was either at ball games or hanging out with Charles and Gary. When I had the time, I fished with Sam.

I loved summer league baseball. The trouble with playing center field, however, is the tendency to stare up at the stars and wonder if somewhere up there someone else is standing in center field staring up at the stars and wondering the same thing. When I wasn't preoccupied with that, I was usually concentrating on equally important matters like whether or not my uniform looked good and was my cap on straight, and why do all the cute girls live in Windthorst or Holliday? Inevitably, just when I'd become totally engrossed in one thought or the other, I'd hear the *crack* of the bat and be overcome with sheer panic until I finally located the ball and determined if it was anywhere near me or not—an occurrence that was foreign to Mickey Mantle or Willie Mays, I'm sure, but happened to me quite often.

My two most vivid memories of those ball-playing days are not of super catches or game-winning homers, but of events that happened within days of each other and resulted only in my reaching first base. The first took place in Archer in a game against Holliday. Sammy Milam was pitching for Holliday, and there was only one other pitcher within a thousand miles that could throw the ball as hard as him, and that was Danny Joe

Schroeder in Windthorst. That night, in my first two at bats, I'd done what most of the team had managed to do against Sammy, which was strike out. Then, just before my third at bat, Coach Mike called me over. "Jim, I think I've finally got this guy figured out. I don't think he can pitch to left-handed batters. [We didn't have any.] I think if you get up there and bat from the other side, he'll walk you—and we need you on base. Whadda you say?"

I was a little nervous because Sammy had only one good eye, but I decided to do my part for the team. "Sure, it's worth a try," I responded.

Bad decision.

Coach Mike was right. He walked me on four straight pitches—the last one a fastball at about a hundred miles an hour that hit me flush in the ribs on my right side before I even had time to blink. I remember thinking I had read somewhere that a kid had died after being hit with a baseball and wondering how that could happen. Now I knew. Nonetheless, I got up, convinced everyone I was fine, and left for first base. I should have kept going.

Two nights later, in Windthorst, with you know who on the mound, I was awaiting my second at bat and running my hand over the spot on my right side the size of a grapefruit and the color of a bad apple, when Coach Mike walked over.

"You know, I think I've just located a chink in Danny's armor. I think he's plumb scared to pitch anyone inside. I'll bet if a fella was to crowd the plate a little, he could get good wood on an outside pitch. Whadda you think?"

I couldn't tell him what I *really* thought. Instead, I said, "I don't know, Coach. Danny seems awfully competitive. Crowding the plate might not set too well with him."

"Quiet and shy as he is? Naw, I gotta believe I done found

his Achilles' heel. I think we got him now, I really do. How 'bout it?"

I hesitated.

"Come on. We're only a couple of runs behind. We can win this thing."

"Okay," I said reluctantly. "At least if he does hit me, it'll be on my other side," I joked.

Bad joke.

I walked to the plate, knocked the dirt from my cleats with the bat, took my stance way inside, and waited. I didn't have to wait long. Danny Joe was having no part of anyone laying claim to the inside part of the plate. His first pitch, a sidearm fastball (more closely resembling a guided missile) hit me flush in my ribs on my left side. Lightning, literally, had struck me twice in three days. I again managed to somehow wind up on first base (although I had no recollection of how I got there). It was then I spotted her. Sitting in the bleachers behind home plate. Blond hair and big brown eyes. *Ingrid Bergman* in cutoffs and flip-flops. And a T-shirt with big block letters that read BEREND BROS. HOG FARM—WINDTHORST, TEXAS. She was sort of skinny and absolutely the most beautiful thing I had ever seen in thirteen years of walking this planet. I remember hoping she thought I was brave for getting up and taking my base without crying. I sure thought I was.

I couldn't take my eyes off of her. Later, when my third at bat came, I strode to the plate, took a couple of ferocious practice swings, pretended to knock the dirt from my cleats, took my stance in the batter's box, and struck out. For vanity's sake, I argued the last called strike with the ump, claiming it was low. He said I was mistaken, and he was probably right, since the darn thing went by so fast I never got a good look at it.

I kept my eyes on her all night (and of course panicked at

each crack of the bat when I was in the outfield). After the game, I went directly to Danny Joe.

"Nice pitching," I said.

"Thanks. You okay?"

"Yeah. Can't you throw any harder than that?" I kidded.

"Sure," he said.

"*That's* scary," I admitted.

He smiled. "I saw your coach talking to you before you batted. I figured that's what he had up his sleeve."

"Yeah. His coaching strategy is going to get me killed one of these days."

We laughed. "Listen, I was wondering . . . do you know who the blonde was sitting behind home plate?"

"Sure," he said. "That's my cousin, Loretta Lu."

"*Loretta Lu?*" I asked.

"We all call her Lorrie," he said, smiling.

"Thank goodness," I said.

"In fact, here she comes now," he said, looking over my shoulder.

He wasn't kidding.

"Hi, Danny," she said as she walked up. "Good game."

"Thanks," he said. "We were just talking about you."

"That so?"

"Yeah." He winked at me and smiled. "Well, good luck!" And off he went.

I watched him go, took a deep breath, and turned. "Hi," I managed.

She studied me for a moment before answering. "Yes?"

"I understand your name is Lorrie."

"So?"

"I understand you and Danny Joe are cousins."

"Most everyone in Windthorst are cousins." (Since only

about four hundred people lived there, and most seemed to have the same last name, she was probably right.) I smiled, but she didn't. This was going to be tougher than I'd thought.

"He's got quite a fastball," I said, lightly rubbing my rib cage.

"You shouldn't have been crowding the plate," she answered.

I laughed, but she didn't.

Enough was enough. Even if it *was* Ingrid Bergman. "Well, goodbye," I said.

She said nothing. I turned to walk away.

"You going to tell me your name, or not?" she asked.

I stopped and turned around. "Jim Black," I said.

"I know that," she answered.

"Then why'd you ask?"

"Just wanted to be sure *you* knew."

I paused for a moment, trying to figure her out. I couldn't. But one thing was for sure. I wasn't going to be knocked down twice in Windthorst in one night.

"Yeah, well, here's something else I know. You sat in something, 'cause you've got a big spot on your rear end." There, take *that*.

She turned, saw it, and looked back at me. Then she did it. She really did. She smiled.

I walked back over.

"You're pretty," I said. I really *was* getting brave.

"You're weird," she replied.

"We belong together."

"Excuse me?"

"You'll see. Someday, you'll see."

"I don't think so."

We stood for a moment looking at each other.

"Well, I have to go," she said.

"Will I see you again?"

"The season's only half over," she answered.

"Then I guess I will."

"I guess," she said, and she turned and walked away.

I watched her go and then called after her.

"Is it true what they say about girls from Windthorst—that you flat out know how to kiss?" I asked.

She stared at me for a second, then answered, "You're weird." And she was gone.

Chapter 16

CHARLES GOT HIMSELF an Eagle. A white Cushman Eagle (my Husky was red) with a padded passenger seat (mine wasn't). We were set. We rode everywhere together. I always felt I looked pretty good on mine. My posture wasn't the greatest, so I figured with the sunglasses I pretty much looked like Marlon Brando. Charles, on the other hand, always appeared a little stiff on his. He had this really great posture (probably from growing up in a house with seven women) that made him look a little like how I thought Fred Astaire might look if he rode a Cushman. Gary must have noticed this, too, because when he went with us, he usually rode with me—even though he had to bring a small pillow off his mom's couch to sit on. That certainly didn't help my Wild One image, but was probably less damaging to it than the way he rode. My Husky also didn't have passenger foot pegs, so Gary would simply dangle his feet to each side. Well, almost immediately he burned his leg on the exhaust pipe. To avoid repeating, he held his legs straight out to the sides as far as he could get them. I finally convinced him that this did not give us the look we were after, so he began holding them out about halfway and bending his knees so that his feet were mere inches from the road. This looked better and worked fine until his legs got tired, then his feet would slowly drop down until suddenly one would contact the road and quite abruptly be knocked back into the air. I had this happen to me once, and it hurts pretty good as well as scaring the daylights out of you. Needless to say, Gary's passenger stints that summer resulted in an assortment of burns, bumps, bruises, and sprains. All in the name of style.

After we tired of riding up and down the streets of Archer trying to impress the girls, we would ride out to the country roads, which we usually had to ourselves. We loved to ride at night under the stars. The night skies of rural Archer County in 1966 were something to behold. Light pollution hadn't yet been invented. Even on moonless nights, there was almost enough starlight to navigate by without headlights (a great sensation).

Our favorite spots, of course, were the places of lore. Legendary scary locations. We were never sure exactly what, if anything, had transpired at the these sites in the past—that depended on who you talked to and when. Here's pretty much what we did know:

At Devil's Drop, west of town, someone had died in a fiery crash when they attempted the drop going way too fast late one night years ago.

At the Old Iron Bridge, north of town, someone had died when a harmless high school prank got out of hand late one night years ago.

At Sleepy Hollow, south of town, someone had died from sheer fright after he saw something while changing a flat tire there late one night years ago.

That said, you'd think we'd do most of our riding *east* of town. We didn't. While the details of these stories were subject to change, it was common knowledge that the restless souls of the victims frequented the sites often. And we were okay with restless souls. We knew them to be horrific, but slow-moving. Which is good. You can get away from a slow mover. The walking dead, mole people, and mummies are good examples. What you want to watch out for is anything that's part animal or really big. Werewolves and spiders or ants the size of houses are examples of these. We hadn't learned this firsthand, mind you, but from Gary's *Famous Monsters* magazines. Same difference.

And then there are those found in *True Detective* magazine. These are worse because they can appear normal. If you keep a keen eye, though, you'll be okay. Usually if they are carrying a long-handled ax, meat cleaver, or red-hot poker, you'd best steer clear.

That's why the rides on our Cushmans were so much fun. In a car, you can roll up the windows and lock the doors. Not so on a scooter. On a scooter, your only hope for survival rests entirely with the skill and daring of the driver. And Charles's and mine must have been pretty good back then, because the three of us did, in fact, always somehow manage to survive.

Chapter 17

I THINK MY MOM'S PATIENCE with Charles, Gary, and myself stemmed from years of working the pediatric floor at Methodist Hospital in Lubbock. Maybe seeing so many sick and dying kids makes you look at your own in a different light. I don't know. I do know she was not overly protective or strict back then. I really think she just wanted us to enjoy the privilege of being kids, and I've always loved her for that. It was easier back then, too, because times were different. In our small town, we really did sleep with doors unlocked and windows open. I know now those were the best of times.

Gary's mom was the only one of our three mothers who had remarried, and we all liked Benny. He was a good guy. And we liked his Fina gas station. Particularly the novelty machine located in the men's restroom. It had some weird stuff. Most items were guaranteed to "drive women crazy," and some were even imported from places like France and Mexico. There was also a condom machine, but Charles was the only one of us brave enough to buy one. Not only that, he put it in his billfold and carried it everywhere. "Never know when you're going to need one," he used to say. However, it would be quite a few more summers before any such "need" actually presented itself.

Today, Gary was at the station working when Charles and I stopped by to get some gas for our mowers.

"Any good new novelty items?" I asked.

"Nope," he replied with a sigh. "May even have to take out the machines."

"How come?" we asked in unison.

"The Baptists are upset. One of the deacons came by and talked to Benny about it."

"Probably wanted to *buy* something," Charles said with a smirk.

"They seem to think it's corrupting our town's youth and encouraging wild, uninhibited sex. That's what he told Benny."

"In *Archer City?*" I asked.

"I'd like to *find* some of that wild, uninhibited sex," Charles said, smiling.

We all laughed.

"Still, Benny wants to do what's right, so I don't know if we'll keep them or not."

"Well, then you might as well just give us some of that watered-down gas y'all sell so we can go cut some grass," I kidded.

Gary filled our cans, and we were on our way. Usually, we could get one of our moms or one of Charles's sisters to give us a ride, but today we had to go it alone. It was quite a ways to Mrs. Poole's house on the north side of town, and it was already hot. Near a hundred. When we got there, she came running out waving her arms.

Mrs. Poole was in her eighties, but she got around really good. She lived by herself and still drove wherever she went. We paused to see what she wanted.

"Hi, boys. I know you're anxious to get started 'fore it gets any hotter, but I need to show you something. This is Buddie," she said as she reached down and straightened a small cross made from Popsicle sticks at my feet. "Buddie died day 'fore yesterday, and here he lays. I would appreciate it if you took extra caution in mowing around him."

"Yes, ma'am," Charles said. "We can do that."

"Was Buddie your cat?" I asked.

"Oh, heavens, no! I wouldn't have a mean ol' cat. Buddie was a parakeet. Still is, I suppose. But he died. Got out of his cage and made a beeline for the picture window. Crashed right into it and passed away. It's a shame, too. He was more than just good company—he was a performer as well. He could whistle or sing most any song—gospel, that is. I'd play the piano, and he'd accompany me. I wanted him to try out for the church choir, but they wouldn't let him. Said it would be distracting. Can you imagine? The way *they* sing? I even made him a choir robe. I wish you boys could've seen him in it."

Neither of us answered.

"Oh well, I'm keeping you from your work, and it's hot. You best get started. I'm sorry to go on like that. I just miss him, that's all." And she smiled and walked back to the house.

Charles and I looked at each other. "She's a sweet lady," I said.

"I know," he answered. "I just wonder if he's buried in that outfit." I laughed and we started our mowers. Her grass was really tall, and it was slow going. We finally finished in about an hour. It seemed like three. She invited us in.

"Would you boys like some fresh fried fish?" she asked.

I was somewhere near heat exhaustion and hot fried fish was the *last* thing I wanted. Charles must have felt the same way. "No thank you," he said. "But we sure could go for some iced tea if you have it."

"*Sure* I do," she said. "Just made it."

We stood in her kitchen and drank nearly that whole pitcher of tea. After we cooled off, we felt better, and the fish was starting to smell really good. "I might try some of that fish, after all," I said.

"I believe I will, too," Charles added.

"Well, you boys help yourselves," and she uncovered a platterful. It tasted as good as it smelled. We ate six or seven pieces each.

"This is delicious," Charles said. "Who caught these catfish for you?"

"Oh, those aren't catfish," she replied. "They're carp. All I eat is carp."

Charles and I looked at each other. "I didn't think carp were fit to eat," I said.

"They're not, if you don't know how to fix them," she said. "Most people don't, but I seem to have a knack."

"What's the secret?" Charles asked.

"It's all in the way you prepare them—it's really very simple. First, you cut off their heads. Then you put them in plastic bags and hang them by the tail on the clothesline till they're good and drained. That's the secret."

We looked at each other again.

"On the clothesline outside?" I asked.

"Oh yes. I couldn't have them hanging in the *house*."

"What are the plastic bags for?"

"To keep the flies off them."

"And just how long do you let them hang out there in this heat?" Charles asked nervously.

"Three days."

We looked at each other for the last time. Thank you, Mrs. Poole. We'd better go."

"*Katy*. Please call me *Katy*."

"Thank you, Katy." And out the door we went.

"But you boys haven't been paid yet!" she called after us.

"That's okay," we called back. "You can pay us next time."

We hadn't gone far when Charles said, "Are you thinking what I'm thinking?"

"Yep. We're probably gonna get sick. *Real* sick. Or worse."

"The way I see it, there's only two things we can do," he said. "We can stop right here, stick our fingers down our throats, and hope it's not too late. Or we can take our chances." And so we left all of that fish and iced tea in the ditch at the corner of N. Mulberry and W. Cherry and continued on down the road. After all, when you're only thirteen and your whole life hangs in the balance, you can't afford to take chances with the likes of food poisoning.

We walked, pushing our mowers for a couple of blocks, before Charles said what was on both our minds. "You know what's crazy? That *really was* good fish."

I looked at him, and we laughed. He was right. It really was.

Chapter 18

I LOVED LISTENING to Sam talk about baseball. Sometimes, when the river was too low to fish, I'd walk down to their house and we'd sit on the porch and talk, and Rose always had something for us to eat, and iced tea or cold Cokes to drink. Rose's cookies, cakes, and pies were out of this world. Her homemade vanilla ice cream was the best there ever was. Period. Sometimes she would sit with us on the porch and sew or knit, but usually she remained in the house, and she always seemed to be singing. She had this wonderful low voice that was just made for gospel hymns, and I loved to sit and talk to Sam and listen to her at the same time.

Sam's love of baseball showed when he talked about it. It was not unlike my dad's. I remember he used to love to watch the New York Yankees on TV. Sam loved to talk about the Negro Leagues, especially the Kansas City Monarchs. Sam's heroes weren't Mantle or Maris or Berra, but he liked to talk about them just the same. And I loved to listen.

"Who was your favorite player, besides Satch?" I asked, reaching for another of Rose's funnel cakes.

Sam took a bite of his and a swig of iced tea. Then he smiled. "That'd be 'Powder Keg' Johnson," he answered. "We called him Powder for short. He was a giant of a man—stood six and one-half feet tall and carried nearly three hundred pounds."

"How'd he get that name?" I asked.

"Well, I never knew if it was because he could hit the ball so far or because he had such a bad temper. But one thing's for sure—no one ever hit the ball like him and most likely never will." Sam handed Tick the Dog his last bite before wiping his hands on his trousers. I anxiously waited for him to continue.

"One time I seen him toss a ball in the air and hit it so hard it shattered a Coke bottle perched on a fence post thirty feet away. I doubt if there's a big-leaguer today who could even hit the bottle, much less break it. And in batting practice, with the pitcher groovin' strikes to him, he routinely hit line drives that broke stadium seats in center field. That is, whenever some-body was brave enough or dumb enough to throw strikes to him," he said with a grin. "But he was at his best against a good fastball pitcher. Knocked balls out of every park he ever played in. And one time in Memphis, he hit a fastball off 'Blinker' Williams that two thousand folks will swear was whistlin' when it left the stadium. I'm one of 'em. That poor ball landed in some feller's garden nearly a block away. They say it traveled nine hundred feet." He paused. "Yessir, Powder was the best hitter I ever saw—shoulda been in the big leagues. Now, *that* woulda been somethin' to see."

"Why didn't he make it?" I asked. "Was it just because he was black?"

"No, son. You see, he had this one little problem. He couldn't stand white folks. Not at all."

"Yeah, that might have been a problem, all right." I smiled.

"After a game once, some feller asked him how he was able to hit the ball so hard. He wanted to know if it was because of his mighty arms, or huge hands, or maybe his powerful legs. Powder's answer was, 'Because it's white.' Needless to say, not too many pro scouts came around after that." Sam chuckled.

I watched Sam closely for a moment and then asked him, "Did you ever feel that way?"

"No, son, I never did. For one reason." He took a long drink of his tea and set the glass down on the porch at his feet. The rings left by the moisture of the glass intertwined and reminded me of the Olympic flag. "When I was about your age, my daddy was arrested for stealin' from and settin' fire to the drugstore in the town where we lived. Some young white boys, a little older than yourself, said they'd seen him runnin' from the store just before it went up. The town was 'bout ready to hang him, it seemed. Then one day one of them boys walked into the jailhouse and told the sheriff how *they'd* done it. How they had been drunk and all, and that my daddy had nothin' to do with it. When all was said and done, they let my daddy go. And that's what he always preached to me—just do what's right. And that's what I've always tried to do. And anytime I started feelin' like Powder, I just remembered that young white boy." He paused. "Besides, Rose won't allow anything less."

Just then her voice drifted out to the porch as she sang:

> *"There's a river up in heaven I shall see someday,*
> *It's the river up in heaven where the children play,*
> *And we shall sit together, hand in hand, I pray,*
> *On the banks of that river someday."*

I listened, enjoying, but didn't recognize the hymn. I looked over at Sam.

"Sometimes she just makes up her own."

I smiled at him and took a drink of tea. I noticed Tick the Dog had moved and was now sitting next to me, watching me eat. "Okay if I give him a piece?" I asked.

"Sure. Just don't let Rose catch you," he said, and grinned.

I glanced toward the screen door and, not taking any chances, quickly gave him my last bite. After swallowing it, he turned and walked back over next to Sam and lay down.

"Where did you meet Rose?" I asked.

"Birmingham," he answered. "I's playin' ball there one day, and she was sellin' hot dogs. Went lookin' for her after the game, but she was gone. Thought I'd missed my chance. Anyhow, the next mornin' I did somethin' I rarely did back then—I went to church. I hadn't been swingin' the bat that good and thought it couldn't hurt. Well, I walked in and there she was—singin' in the choir. I couldn't take my eyes off her. Didn't hear a thing that preacher said, and when he finished, I went straight up there, told her my name, and asked what hers was. She said Rosella, and I told her that she was pretty as a rose." He paused.

"What happened then?" I asked.

"I hung around for a while, and she eventually sent me on my way. Never said why, exactly. I always guessed it was because I was gone so much playin' ball. Anyway, truth is, she broke my heart."

"Then how did you wind up together?"

"Nearly twenty years passed 'fore I saw her again. I'd been outta baseball for some time and down on my luck, and was just comin' back. I's determined to turn things around, and was doin' so, but knew somethin' was missin'. On a hunch, I went back to Birmingham, back to that little church, and there she was—still singin' in the choir, and still pretty as a rose. We been together ever since."

"That's a heck of a story," I said.

"That it is, son. That it is."

"But how'd you wind up here?"

"Well, she was ready to get out of Alabama and had always wanted to see Texas, so we came. Jobs were hard to come by, so we just kept movin'. I'd caught some fish in this here river and was in town tryin' to sell 'em when Mr. Coot came by and asked if I be interested in cleanin' his barbershop. One thing led to another, and we been right here ever since."

"You have any kids?" I asked.

"No, son, we never did. We wanted some. She wanted a houseful. It just never happened for us."

He looked away for a moment. "I tell you, that woman don't have what she deserves. Don't have much at all, in fact, and I'm to blame for that. And why she still loves me the way she does, I guess I'll never know. But I do know this—she'll never know how much I love *her*. No one could." He looked down at the ground for a second, then back up at me. "Son, there's just nothin' like lookin' at the woman you love with all your soul and seein' that love shinin' in her eyes. Nothin' like it in this whole world, I tell ya. Nothin'."

Chapter 19

ON A CLEAR, HOT JULY NIGHT in the summer of 1966, the stars fell from the sky and landed in Archer City. That summer brought us one of the best meteor showers ever, and with it a unique opportunity. That night, we reached a whole other level of accomplishment and a new plateau in prank hierarchy.

"I can't believe I let you guys talk me into this," Gary whispered. "I swear I must really be crazy after all."

"What do you mean, *you guys?* This was Bubba's idea," Charles whispered back.

"Heck it was!" I said, a little too loudly. They both whirled and grimaced at me.

"Will you be quiet? Someone's gonna hear us!"

We peered over the ledge and looked down at the street. Parked in front of the Golden Rooster Restaurant were cars belonging to the sheriff, his deputy, and the night watchman, who were all inside eating. From atop the Archer County Courthouse, we could see for miles, but our targets, and our concern, were the three individuals finishing up their cobbler and coffee.

"I still don't trust Charles to do the shooting," Gary was saying.

"Do *you* want to?" he replied.

"No way! What if we get caught?"

"You'll still be an accessory," Charles said.

Gary looked down at the sack of lava rocks in his lap that Charles had borrowed from his granddad's outdoor barbeque grill. "I can't *believe* I let you guys talk me into this. What was I thinking?"

I glanced down at the propane torch bottle I was holding, then over at the slingshot in Charles's hand.

"It's time!" he said.

I peered over the ledge again and saw Sheriff Harris; Don, the deputy; and Zeke, the night watchman, standing on the sidewalk fiddling with an assortment of toothpicks, breath mints, and cigarettes. We strained to hear.

"That's *some* cobbler, that's all I got to say about it," Don was saying.

"It'll do in a pinch," Sheriff Harris answered.

"I think I chipped a tooth on mine," Zeke added.

"Hell, Zeke, there ain't no seeds in peach cobbler," the sheriff told him.

"Well, there sure as hell was somethin' in it, and I prefer to think it was a seed of some sort. Otherwise, I might get sick thinkin' about it."

Just then a brilliant falling star streaked across the sky, right on schedule. We couldn't have asked for more.

"Did y'all see that?" Don exclaimed.

"I missed it," Zeke said. "What was it?"

"A fallin' star. There's a meteor shower tonight."

"Let's do it!" Charles declared.

"Oh shit," Gary said, putting on his mother's best cooking mitts. He then reached into his sack and pulled out a lava rock about the size of a golf ball and held it out. I lit the torch, adjusted the flame, and held it up to the rock. Soon as the rock was glowing red, Gary handed it to Charles, who wore heavy work gloves. He loaded the slingshot and waited for just the right moment.

"There goes another one!" Don announced.

Charles aimed for the middle of Main Street and let fly. The rock hit just there and skidded toward the group. It came to rest under the sheriff's car.

"What the hell was that?" one of them said.

"I don't know."

Another falling star above us.

I heated, Gary handed, and Charles launched. This one two-hopped and hit the bumper on Don's cruiser.

They all three flinched, then stood staring at the object in the street before them.

"What the hell?"

Zeke walked over, studied it for a moment, then reached down to pick it up. He shouldn't have.

"Son of a bitch!" he yelled as he flung the rock. *"Burnt the shit outta me!"*

The sheriff and Don looked at each other.

Charles's third shot bounced off the roof of Don's car and hit him square in the chest.

"Damn!" he yelled, jumping backward, arms flailing. The three of them studied it lying there before them. It was smoking.

"What the hell *is* that?" one of them asked again.

Zeke walked over with his. It had cooled enough for him to hold. "Fallin' star," he said, holding it out.

The other two looked at it, then down at the one at Don's feet. He reached down and lightly touched it. It was still warm. "Damn sure is," he said. "A meteor for sure!"

"Well, I'll be," the sheriff said, shaking his head. "Now, ain't that somethin'?"

A few more people wandered out of the restaurant, having watched the goings-on from inside. The first out was Clifford

McFarland, a local rancher. "What the hell's all the dancin' around out here about, Sheriff? Buffalo gnats gettin' you fellas?"

"Hell no, but the meteors are," Don answered. "Damn things are hittin' all over out here."

"Meteors? Have you boys been—"

Charles's next shot was too good to be true. It knocked Clifford's Stetson off his head and somehow managed to wind up inside it on the sidewalk.

"Damn!" he yelled. "What was *that?*"

"A meteor!" Zeke exclaimed. "Are you deaf?"

Clifford reached down, picked up his hat, and put it on.

"Hell's bells!" he yelled again as he jerked his hat off and waved it wildly. The rock flew out. Everyone stood staring at it smoking on the sidewalk. Clifford was rubbing the top of his bald head. "Hell, you weren't kidding!" he said, just as his wife came out the door. "Get back inside, sweetie! The whole sky's fallin'."

They all scrambled back inside. Some watched through the plate-glass window, while others examined the top of Clifford's head.

We were nearly hysterical, and laughing so hard we were crying. My side was killing me. Gary was sucking on his inhaler. I was about to ask him if I could borrow it when his face turned bright red as did everything else around us. *Glowing red.* We turned and saw the large auto flare Charles had secretly taped to the antenna tower a few feet away, burning brightly. I whirled and looked down at the restaurant. Inside, they were all looking up and pointing in our direction. We were lit up like a Christmas tree. And Charles was gone.

Chapter 20

THE ROOF OF THE Archer County Courthouse is covered
with Mexican-style rounded baked clay shingles that are slick
as all get-out and difficult enough to navigate without being
pressed for time and having to carry what surely was incrimi-
nating evidence. Charles was already nearly to the fire escape,
the slingshot in his back pocket. I had a more difficult time with
the propane torch, the tip of which was still plenty hot. Gary,
however, had an almost impossible task. He was trying to cross
the tiles still wearing his mother's oven mitts, the sack of lava
rocks hanging from his mouth. It was too much. He yelled, and
I turned and watched him sliding tractionless toward the edge
of the roof. He had closed his eyes in anticipation of his seem-
ingly inevitable fate, and I was about to do the same. Then, in
one of the great unsolved mysteries of all time, he came to a
stop at the last instant. Who knows what undefined force was
holding him to that roof? It certainly wasn't a law of nature.
Perhaps his sheer will, and nothing more.

He opened his eyes.

"Hang on," I said as I made my way toward him.

He looked up, afraid to speak.

"Lift one of your hands up for a second," I told him.

He did, and I tugged off one mitt, then the other. With his
hands now free, he began to pull himself up. I put his gloves under one arm and the torch under the other and started back up.
He followed me over the roof to the stairs. When we reached
the ground, Charles was waiting.

"What kept you guys?" he half whispered.

"Gary almost died," I said.

"Well, we're all going to if we don't get outta here," he said.

We took off across the lawn and raced toward the dark surrounding Tom's Boot Repair Shop across the street. A block away, we could hear the screeching of tires. We started our Cushmans, and the race was on.

Down alleys. Up side streets. Without lights. As close to reckless abandon as the three of us had ever been. Minutes later, we were headed up Ash Street past the school and toward the golf course. The law was just three blocks behind and closing as I pulled up beside Charles.

"What about the dip?" I yelled.

"What?" he yelled back.

"The diiiiip! Up ahead!"

"Jump it!" he shouted back.

It was a block ahead and coming up fast. I turned my head and yelled back to Gary, *"Hang on!"*

Charles hit it first. We watched as he bottomed out loud and hard and went airborne. There wasn't enough time to see how and where he landed before it was our turn.

At the last instant, I became fully aware of what a terrible error in judgment we'd committed. Then we hit the bottom of the dip hard and bounced forward and upward. I was certain Gary and the rear end of the scooter were passing overhead, and they almost did. Somehow, he managed to hold on and slammed back down hard on the passenger seat (and I mean *hard*, because he'd forgotten to bring his mother's couch pillow). I somehow managed to keep us upright and noticed Charles had also survived. We sped on down the road, made two turns, and headed out the Olney highway. A mile up it, once over the hill, we pulled off into a wheat field and killed the engines. I was certain they had seen us turn off, but instead, our pursuers raced on by.

We got off the bikes. Gary hadn't spoken since the court-house roof. "You okay?" I asked.

He was walking like John Wayne. "You guys are crazy," he said. "We could've all been killed." He groaned and rubbed his rear end and his crotch. "I don't think I'll ever be able to have kids or sit up straight again."

"You wouldn't have anyway if the sheriff had caught us," Charles offered. "None of us would have."

"Think they know who did it?" I asked.

"I doubt it. I don't think they ever got a good look at us." He looked around. "Where are the lava rocks?" he asked.

"I think they're in the rain gutter," I answered.

"On the *courthouse?*"

"Yep. And don't say another word," Gary challenged. "When I was back there hanging on for dear life, they were not high on my list. If you want 'em, go get 'em."

Charles and I smiled. "Naw, they'll probably be okay there," he said. "Even if they do find them, you didn't leave any fingerprints—you were wearing the oven mitts. We should be in the clear."

Just then, the three cars topped the hill, heading back, sirens blaring. Our hearts stopped. We ducked low, and they roared past, toward town. Soon it was quiet again.

"Well, just how many kids in town have Cushmans? Did you think of that? I sure as heck wish you had before you lit that flare."

"You shoulda seen the look on y'all's faces," Charles said, laughing.

"Gary almost died up there. I'm serious," I reminded him.

"If I'd known we were gonna hit that dip like we did, I'd

probably have just let go back there on the roof," Gary said. "Can a person get hemorrhoids from something like that?"

We were all laughing now.

"You'll be okay," Charles said.

"Maybe," Gary replied, "but I know one thing—I'm riding home with *you*. And I ain't never gettin' on Jim's again without my pillow."

"I bet we did look funny up in midair like that," I said.

"Yeah, but I still think we should've been able to clear that dip," Charles speculated. "We just needed a little more speed, that's all."

Gary and I both looked at him.

"Okay, well, maybe more than just a little," he confessed.

We laughed.

Our heart rates were returning to near normal for the first time in a while. We sat there on the ground, amid the wheat, and stared up at the sky. Suddenly a huge bright light streaked across before us. The meteor shower was still going on. We lay back on the ground to watch.

Suddenly Gary sat up. "You don't reckon they can identify me if they *do* find that bag of rocks, do you? I mean, I *did* have it in my mouth. There might be teeth marks on it."

"Probably," Charles and I said in unison.

"Thanks a lot," he said.

We lay there in silence, watching in wonder. Soon we had forgotten all about the law and the dip. The meteor show was at its peak, and we had a front-row seat.

Chapter 21

THE FRONT PAGE of the *Archer County News* that week featured a picture of the scab on top of Clifford McFarland's bald head, under which a caption read: *Local citizen injured in meteor storm.* The story went on to say how Archer City had apparently been bombarded with more than its share of falling star fragments in the recent meteor shower; and in what had to be a freak of nature, several fell within just a few feet of each other on Main Street. A second photo showed Archer's three law enforcement officers examining the scene directly in front of the Golden Rooster Restaurant, having witnessed the event firsthand. No mention was made of suspected foul play.

We agreed to take it easy for a while with meteors and such, having decided not to press our luck. We did receive some notoriety from our friends about it, despite not having told a soul. Funny how word gets around.

And so we settled back into our routines. Charles still mowed with me but had taken on another part-time job with a local ditching service. Gary still helped Benny at the Fina station and continued to work on building one of the finest collections of *True Detective* and *Famous Monsters* magazines ever assembled. I mowed, played ball, and fished.

On this particular day, I stopped by the Fina to kill some time on my way to the river. Gary was washing some gal's windshield and sneaking glances at her legs, which he thought went undetected but was mistaken. It seemed to take him forever. When he finished, he walked over.

"You hear the news?" he asked.

"No, what?"

"The Klan killed Kennedy," he said, somber-faced.

"The Klan? Who says?"

"Jesse. He and Roy just left here."

"How does *he* know?"

"Says his dad told him they done it. Seems they were upset with all that civil rights stuff."

"His dad's been dead for twenty years."

"Jesse says his dad still visits him on important matters."

"You believe that?"

"Heck no," he said. "But I ain't gonna argue with him."

Jesse and Roy were regulars at Benny's Fina. They hadn't completely lost their minds yet, but Jesse was getting close. Friends since grade school, and long since retired, they spent each day leaned against the outside of the bank, post office, courthouse, and Fina station—rotating every couple of hours from one to the other. Usually Jesse just whittled while Roy whistled, but occasionally they talked. I must admit, they were fun to listen to, but sometimes could get on your nerves. Especially Jesse. And this particular time, he struck an unpleasant chord with me. Kennedy's death still upset me after three years, and talk of it stirred a familiar feeling which I greatly disliked. It made me remember where I was when it happened, and certain sights and sounds from that day that were still clear in my mind.

I remember I was standing on the playground, leaning against the backstop waiting for my turn at bat, when some kid ran by and said the president had been shot in the head. The bell rang, and we returned to our fifth-grade class. It was a few minutes before Mrs. Hayes walked in. She was in her fifties and wore really thick glasses. Through them, it was easy to see she had been crying. She was still sobbing when she spoke.

"Class, something terrible has happened. Our president has been shot. I think you will understand if we do not continue class. Instead, let's each just place our heads on our desks and quietly deal with this tragedy in our own way." Then she walked over to her desk, laid her head down, and wept.

Eventually, everyone put their heads down, and soon it became quiet except for the sound of her sobbing and that of Gary Silsby's at the rear of the class. Gary was new in school and was from up north somewhere. He was pretty much thought to be a sissy by most of the guys. This didn't help his image.

After a while, they had ceased crying, and the room was silent, when suddenly someone clambered out of his chair and started walking toward the front. Whoever it was wore cowboy boots and dragged the heels across the old hardwood floors, making a terrible racket. I hadn't looked up yet when he stopped up front near the door. It was quiet again for a second, and then there was the most god-awful sound of someone clearing his nose and throat, a loud spit, and the unmistakable sound of something banging into the metal trash can. Everyone looked up.

The culprit started back to his seat.

"Lawrence?" Mrs. Hayes said.

He stopped.

"What was that?" she asked.

"What?" he answered.

"What was that you deposited in the wastepaper basket?"

He didn't miss a beat. Rather, he hooked his thumbs into the pockets of his jeans, shrugged his shoulders, and answered, "Snot."

There were some scattered chuckles from around the room.

"Pardon me?" she asked.

He shrugged his shoulders again. "Snot."

More laughter.

She stood up and walked over to him. "Lawrence Brown, you pick up that can and take it down to Mr. Wallace's office right now. I'll be along in a moment."

Whatever smile he had faded. "Ma'am?"

"You heard me. Now go on."

The room was quiet. He was always getting her goat. But maybe not this time. He picked up the can.

"Go on," she said.

He walked out into the hall and paused just outside the door, and just out of her sight, but still within view of his buddies. He shrugged his shoulders again, and began shooting her the finger.

"Class, I'll be right back. Please continue our show of respect for the president," she said before walking out. Larry heard her coming just in time and headed down the hall. She followed close behind. Kennedy had just been shot, and everyone around me was laughing and talking. It just didn't seem right.

I looked up now and spotted Roy and Jesse returning. All this crap about the Klan wasn't right, either. Even if it had been three years since his death. I had to speak up—something I didn't do back then. I was about to confront Jesse when Roy delivered his own analysis.

"That Klan talk is a buncha shit, and you know it. Hell, we all know who killed the president. It was them damn Russkies. Everyone knows that."

"Don't they live over near Holliday?" Jesse wanted to know.

"You nitwit. I'm talkin' about the damn USSR. Everyone knows they were embarrassed and pissed at Kennedy over that blockade business. Hell, he might as well have just pulled their britches down for everyone to see."

"Come to think of it, I kinda remember that," Jesse was saying. "Had something to do with missiles, didn't it?"

"Hell yes," Roy responded.

Jesse paused, thinking. "Had that James Bond feller in it."

Roy's face suddenly turned bright red. "I ain't talkin' 'bout no movie!"

"Oh," Jesse answered quietly.

"Lord have mercy!"

Jesse turned and walked away. "I better tell Pa about this."

"I would if I's you!" Roy called after him. He watched Jesse for a moment, and then followed after him, mumbling to himself.

Gary rolled his eyes. "Sometimes I think I oughta sell tickets," he said.

"Well, I know one thing," I said. " I hope I never get old. That's for sure."

Chapter 22

GARY AND I WERE ON MY CUSHMAN, stopped at the blinking red light. He was adjusting his mom's pillow when Charles pulled up beside us. He was a mess.

"What the heck happened to you?" I asked. His face was plastered with Band-Aids of all shapes and sizes. Under the dim glow of the streetlights he looked kind of spooky.

"Shingles," he answered with disgust.

"Aren't they contagious?" Gary asked nervously.

"Roofing shingles, you idiot! I got hit in the face with a bunch 'em."

"How?" I asked.

"Helping a neighbor roof his house. A bundle slid off, and I tried to catch it. I didn't know the paper had already been torn off. They got me pretty good."

"I'll say they got you," Gary said. "You look terrible."

"Yeah, you look like something from one of Gary's monster magazines," I kidded.

"Thanks a lot. You guys are great for cheering somebody up."

I laughed and happened to look over his shoulder.

"Oh my gosh!" I said. "Guys, that's her!"

"Who?" they asked.

I pointed to the Royal Theater down the street to our right. "Lorrie!"

"Who?"

"The girl I was telling you about. The one from the ball game. That's her!"

She was with two other girls and a woman who was buying tickets. They went inside.

"Let's go!" I said.

We hurried over and parked our scooters out front. As soon as we stepped up onto the sidewalk, Charles grabbed my arm and stopped. He was looking up at the marquee, where big block letters announced, WALT DISNEY'S BAMBI.

"Hold on, Bubba!" he said.

"Come on, guys," I pleaded. I looked at Gary.

"Nope. I'm with Charles on this. You can see her some other time."

"I'll pay," I said.

They shook their heads.

"Popcorn and Cokes, too. My treat. Whadda you say?"

They looked at each other. "Candy, too?" Gary asked.

I looked in my wallet and did a quick calculation. "Sure," I said.

"Okay," they said in unison but somewhat reluctantly.

I bought the tickets, and we loaded up on goodies at the concession stand. Then we stepped into the tiny dark theater. I headed down the aisle toward some vacant seats a couple of rows behind her. When I stopped to turn into a row, Charles pushed me in the back. He did so until we arrived at her row. "Here," he said.

I looked at him and started toward where Lorrie was sitting. Each time I tried to stop, he pushed harder. Before I knew it, I was right next to her. There was no turning back. I could hardly breathe as I sat down. Charles sat next to me.

The four of them looked over at me. The woman and the other two girls smiled. Then they all looked back up at the screen.

"Hi," I managed.

"Shhhh," she replied. "Watch the movie."

I glanced up. Bugs Bunny was giving Elmer Fudd fits. "It's only the cartoon," I said.

She didn't answer. *Here we go again,* I thought. *This girl might be beautiful, but she definitely needs to work on her communication skills.*

"That your mom?" I asked.

"My Aunt Agnes. And two of my cousins," she answered, staring ahead. "She brings us every Friday night after working in the fields."

"What kind of fields do you work in?"

She turned. "Not us—*her.* Cotton."

"I didn't know there were any cotton fields in Archer County."

"You should get out more often."

I studied the side of her face as she studied the screen. I'd run out of words. The movie began, and I watched it and thought about her.

Toward the end of the movie, I noticed she was crying. So were her cousins and aunt. I soon realized why. Bambi's mother had been shot. I looked over, and Charles was gone. I couldn't see Gary's face for his hand. "Where's Charles?" I asked. Gary shook his head and didn't answer.

I was thankful I had only been staring at the screen blindly. Otherwise I probably would have been bawling. Soon everyone regained their composure, and Charles returned.

"Where'd you go?" I asked.

"Had to go take a leak," he replied.

"*Sure* you did."

"I *did!*" he shot back.

Lorrie looked over at us and frowned. Then, "What happened to your friend's face?"

"Charles? A roofing accident."

"Is he okay?"

"Yeah. His pride's hurt a little right now, that's all."

I thought I detected a trace of a smile, but I wasn't sure. Still, *she* had initiated the conversation. I was encouraged. "You want some popcorn?" I asked

Now she did smile. "Thanks," she replied.

"Here, take it."

"That's sweet of you."

Charles suddenly punched me in the arm, and I winced and whirled around.

"Put your arm around her," he whispered.

I looked over at her. He punched me again.

"Will you quit that?"

"Put your arm around her. She wants you to."

"Are you sure?" I asked. I snuck another quick peek at her. Charles drew back his fist. "Okay, okay!" He put his hand down.

She was watching the movie intently. I slowly placed my arm over the back of her chair. She turned and looked at it. Then went back to watching the movie.

I sat up a little straighter and prouder. I was rolling now.

"I drive a motorcycle," I said. "It's parked outside."

"You do? What kind?" she asked.

"A big Cushman Husky. Red."

"That's not a motorcycle. That's a scooter."

"It's still big," I said. "Gary even rides on the back with me. That is, when he remembers to bring a pillow from his mom's couch."

Oh no, that look. I knew what was coming.

"You are really weird. You know that?" she said.

I wanted to kick myself. I felt my body slump and found my-self staring at the ceiling. I didn't speak again, and when the movie ended, they got up to leave. I stood up. The woman smiled again, and the two girls giggled at me. The four of them stepped out into the aisle. Lorrie turned and looked back. I held my breath.

"Well, don't hurt yourself on that *big* scooter," she said. And she left.

Charles and Gary were howling. "What's so funny?" I asked. "I think she likes me."

"Oh yeah. No question about it," Charles joked.

"Did you kiss her?" Gary wanted to know.

"No. I didn't."

"Hold her hand?"

"No. But I did put my arm around her."

"Well, when are you going out with her?" Charles asked. "You did ask her for a date, didn't you?"

I shook my head, embarrassed. "But I'll see her again. We still have a ball game left to play in Windthorst."

"What are we gonna do with you, Bubba?"

We stepped outside just in time to see the taillights of Aunt Agnes's car disappear over the hill. My heart sank.

Chapter 23

I SAT ALONE in Joe's Drive-in, staring blindly out the window, hoping Lorrie would somehow come through the door, spot me, and walk over. I'd buy her a Coke, play a killer song on the jukebox, and she'd actually put two or more sentences together. Then, of course, we'd hold hands. A figure walked past outside, and it was a moment before I realized it was Sam. I ran after him.

"Sam!"

He paused and cocked his head, listening.

"Sam! It's me!"

He turned, looked my way, and smiled.

I ran over to him. "What are you doing here?" I asked.

"An odd job for a feller up the street. Some folks will pay good money to have the littlest things done."

"Come in and I'll buy you a Coke," I said, and turned away. I'd gone a couple of steps when I realized he hadn't followed. "Are you coming?" I asked.

"I reckon I'll just be gettin' on home."

"Aw, come on. You've got time for a Coke. As many as you and Rose have given me, the least I can do is buy you one. They have the best chocolate Cokes around."

He gave me a funny look.

"I know," I said. "You see, Charles always gets a cherry Coke, Gary likes vanilla in his, and I like chocolate in mine. You should try it. Whadda you say?"

He hesitated and then smiled. "It *is* a might warm out today.

I believe I'll just take you up on that. That is, if I can have mine straight."

We laughed and walked to the door. I opened it and followed him in. "I'm sitting over here," I said. He followed me to my booth and sat down across from me. Alvin Holcomb and a buddy, who were seated in a booth next to the window, were staring at us. Joe walked over.

"Howdy, Samuel. How are you?"

"Real fine, sir."

"And Rose?"

"Mean as ever," he kidded.

"Glad to hear it," Joe said, smiling. He then motioned to me. "Sam, you're aware you're running with a pretty wild fellow here, aren't you?"

Sam smiled and said, "I am a might concerned 'bout my reputation."

We all chuckled.

"What'll it be?"

"I guess a cold Coke Cola would hit the spot."

"Straight," I said.

Joe smiled and left. I glanced over and noticed Alvin and his friend had gone back to eating. A moment later, Joe returned with Sam's drink. "Enjoy," he said, before returning to the kitchen.

"You two friends?" I asked.

"No," Sam answered. "I used to help Joe out with his yard work a few years back till his boy got old enough. He's a nice man."

"Yes, he is," I replied. "You come in here often?"

"Not much," he said.

"No kidding?"

I was just about to ask why when Charles and Gary came

through the door. They spotted me and walked over. Startled, they stopped and looked at Sam.

"Hey, guys, what are you doing here?" I asked.

"We, uh, saw your scooter out front."

Their eyes were focused on me now. "Have you ever met Sam?" I asked.

They shook their heads.

"Sam, these are my friends I've told you about . . . Charles and Gary. Guys, this is Sam."

Sam smiled and nodded. He was as uneasy as they were. They smiled (sort of) and nodded back. No one spoke, and I began to get anxious. Gary looked around the diner. I followed his eyes and discovered, too, that everyone was staring at the four of us. I scooted over and said, "Y'all want to sit down?" Gary looked at Charles and then quickly slid in beside me. Somewhat reluctantly, Charles sat down beside Sam. Joe walked over.

He smiled and said, "Sam, you're gettin' in deeper and deeper."

Sam smiled back. "I don't know. They look like pretty good folk to me."

"That's where they'll get you, if you're not careful," he said with a wink. Then, "the usual for you two?"

Charles and Gary nodded and Joe left.

We sat there in silence, waiting for him to return. Shortly he did. He placed their drinks on the table and left.

After a moment, Gary spoke up. "You two come on your scooter?" he asked.

"No." I grinned. "Just me. Sam used to have one years ago, though, didn't you, Sam?"

"Sure did. I miss it, too."

"Did your wife have to carry a pillow with her?" Gary asked.

Sam chuckled. "Rose? Oh no. She wouldn't get near the thing—never trusted my drivin'. Can't say I blame her, though."

"What'd you ever do with it, Sam?" I asked.

"I finally had to swap it to a feller for some boards and nails I's needin'. It was time, though."

Suddenly there was a loud shout, and we all jumped.

"Hey! Get the hell away from the window, you damn looney bird!"

We looked over. Alvin was tapping on the glass with his knuckle. Outside, Harley stared through the window, face pressed against the glass, hands cupped around his eyes. Right next to where Alvin was sitting.

"Hey! You hear me?"

Joe appeared from the kitchen. We looked at him, then back at the window. Harley was gone.

The front door opened. There was a pause, and then Joe spoke.

"Come in, Harold. Come right on in."

Another moment passed, and Harley shuffled in and over to our booth, where he stood staring at the floor. Joe pulled up a chair for him. Then he went back to the kitchen and Harley sat down.

"Damn, Joe. Don't you have any rules about who you let in here?" Alvin said loudly.

Joe returned carrying a cup of coffee and a straw. "No, Alvin. If I did, you wouldn't be here." He set them in front of Harley and left again. We watched him go, then looked at Harley.

"Hello, Harold," I said.

He didn't respond. Instead, he began sipping the hot coffee through the straw. I thought I heard him say "Ouch" but wasn't sure. "You remember Charles and Gary, don't you?"

He didn't answer. I looked at Sam. "We gave Harold a ride home a while back when it was raining so hard."

"That so?" he replied. "That might be a first. Harold isn't too fond of motor vehicles."

"Because of his crash?" Gary asked.

"Yessir."

"We figured it was because people were mean to him."

"No. Most folks 'round here treat Harold with respect, far as I know."

Charles turned to look at Alvin.

"What are you lookin' at? I'm the only normal person in here!" He paused. "You should see yourselves. You look like a damn circus."

"Sorry about the bad company today, fellas. Drinks on the house," Joe called out from the kitchen.

"What about *me?*" Alvin wanted to know.

"What *about* you?"

"Who's buyin' mine?"

Before Joe could answer, Harley stood up and walked to the register. He placed some money on the counter and, without ever looking up, left. Joe walked over and looked at it.

"I guess there's your answer," he said.

"Bullshit," Alvin said, disbelieving.

"I reckon I'll be goin', too," Sam said, rising.

"Yeah, me, too."

We four thanked Joe and walked outside. Harley was already a ways up the street.

"You all be careful on those scooters, you hear?" Sam said.

"We will. So long, Sam."

"It was nice meetin' you two. Jim here talks an awful lot about you."

"Same here," they answered.

"'Bye, now." He turned in Harley's direction. "Harold! Hold up!" And we watched him walk away. After he was gone, Charles was the first to speak.

"Well, I know one thing . . . I just ate *my* words. I clearly remember telling you I wouldn't be caught dead at any of y'all's tea parties."

Gary was next. "Yeah, I never thought I would, either. I bet I'm the only guy around to get attacked by the Walking Man and then have coffee with him."

"I guess we were quite a sight, all right," I added.

Gary glanced toward the diner. "I don't think Alvin was too happy about it."

"Who *cares* what he thinks?" Charles replied. "Or anybody else, for that matter. Ain't that what you say, Bubba?"

I nodded. Just then, Alvin came out the door. He glared at us and muttered something under his breath as he got in his pickup. Then he backed up, turned around, and peeled out, spraying us with gravel. As he drove away, Charles shot him the finger. But I don't think he could see us for all the dust.

Chapter 24

TO THIS DAY, in documentaries about Bigfoot, a map of the United States is used with markers denoting areas where reported sightings have occurred. If you look closely, you will spot one in north-central Texas approximately where Archer City is situated. Here's why.

Charles, Gary, and I were camped that fateful night on the Little Wichita River northwest of town near the Old Iron Bridge. We were actually camped in the riverbed itself, as it hadn't rained in quite a while and the ground was dry as a bone. Its steep banks provided us good protection from the wind and made for a nice, cozy spot. After we set up camp, we hiked up the riverbed a ways with our pellet rifles, searching for wild game. There was none, so we headed back, stopping to set a small-game steel trap, baited with bacon, about a hundred feet from our bedrolls. Then we cooked supper and laughed and talked until nearly midnight. We were lying on our sleeping bags, half asleep, listening to pop music on the transistor radio, when suddenly Gary sat up. "What was *that?*"

"What?" I replied.

"I heard something," he answered, staring up the riverbed.

"Probably some guy with a hook for a hand hiding in the bushes," Charles said without moving.

"Yeah, or the poor lost soul of one of his victims," I added.

We laughed, and Gary shot us an aggravated glance.

"Very funny." He took one last look around and lay back down. "Is there anything left to eat?" he asked.

"Nope," Charles answered. "You ate it all."

"I sure could go for some chocolate cake right about now."

"Will you stop that?" I said. "Now you're making *me* hungry."

"Why don't you go over there and see if the man with the hook will give you something?" Charles kidded. He and I had just begun to laugh when suddenly there was a loud metallic *whack* just up the riverbed. The three of us sat up. Scared. Charles and I looked at each other.

"I *told* you," Gary whispered.

We reached for our pellet rifles while Gary grabbed the flashlight. When we were ready, we motioned for him to shine the light.

At first we couldn't see anything. He moved the light from side to side. I remember thinking that whatever had sprung our trap better not be *too big*, with our limited firepower. *It was.* There was a reflection of sorts up higher. Gary raised the light, and there they were—a pair of bright orange eyes reflecting back at us from about eight feet above the ground.

Whatever it was, wasn't the least bit happy with the light in its eyes or the trap on its foot. It let out some sort of loud screech and angrily kicked at the trap and chain. We froze. Then suddenly it appeared the eyes were getting closer. *And they were.* Whatever it was, was coming our way. Gary had dropped the light and was already halfway up the bank. Charles and I joined him. It was steep and hard to climb and we felt we might never reach the top alive, but we did, and jumped on our Cushmans. Charles's started right off. Mine didn't. The thing had reached our spot and was trying to climb the bank. It, too, was having a difficult time of it, and wasn't pleased. Finally, my Husky fired, and Gary jumped on, and off we went. I'm not sure how we negotiated that small dirt trail at breakneck speed back to the main road and into town without killing ourselves, but we did.

I dropped Gary off, almost without stopping, and headed home. Charles was a block or two ahead and not looking back. I didn't blame him. Somehow, I, too, made it home.

At seven the next morning, we met at Joe's Drive-in. None of us had slept.

We ordered breakfast and looked at each other. Gary broke the silence.

"What the heck *was* that?"

"I don't know, and don't want to know," I said, rubbing my goose bumps.

"Bigfoot," Charles said calmly.

We both looked at him, but down deep we knew.

It was. It really was. It had to be.

"Who are we going to tell?" Gary asked.

"No one," Charles answered.

Neither of us spoke up.

"Who is there in this whole town that would believe the three of *us*?"

He had a point.

Our breakfasts arrived, and we dug into our eggs, bacon, hash browns, biscuits, toast, pancakes, and coffee. (A Bigfoot sighting works up a big appetite.)

"What are we going to do about our stuff?" Gary wanted to know.

"We're gonna go get it," Charles stated matter-of-factly.

We both looked at him again.

"He's right," I finally said. "We can't just leave it there."

"I don't know," Gary said.

"We'll go at noon. In broad daylight," Charles said. "That thing surely won't be around then. It'll probably be off asleep somewhere."

"Yeah, or eating a cow or something," Gary said, and we laughed.

"Maybe it isn't as big as it looked last night," I offered.

"*It is,*" they both replied.

"Anyway, it might be fifty miles from here by now."

"It very well could be," Charles replied.

"I sure hope so," Gary said.

"On the other hand, it might have gone and gotten the others," Charles said.

"*Others?*" Gary and I had stopped chewing.

"Just kidding." He smiled.

We looked at each other and then up at the clock. It was eight A.M. Four hours till high noon.

Chapter 25

WHEN WE PULLED OUT at 11:59 that morning, I think we were all feeling a little braver. After all, the sun was shining brightly, and we were on a mission. There should have been music playing in the background. Perhaps the theme to *The Searchers*. Or at least *Have Gun, Will Travel*.

Charles had "borrowed" two of his granddad's guns. He kept the shotgun and gave me the .22 rifle. I was glad to have it. We carried them laid across our handlebars. Gary carried a can of his mother's hair spray and a cigarette lighter—a trick he'd recently seen on *Dragnet*. (We hoped it wouldn't come to that.) We took our time through town and down the Seymour highway. It wasn't until we turned onto the Old Iron Bridge Road that I began to get a little nervous. A few miles down the road, once the bridge came into view, it hit me flush in the stomach. I pulled over.

Charles pulled up alongside.

"What's the matter?" he asked.

I looked down the dirt road to the bridge, then back at him. "What the *heck* are we doing?" I said. "We must be *crazy*."

"My thoughts exactly," Gary said from behind me.

Charles looked down the road, then back at us. "Well, what's it gonna be?

Gary and I both thought about it for more than a moment. We looked at each other.

"All right," I said reluctantly.

"I guess," Gary added. "Besides, there might be more to this than we think. It may be out of our hands," he said.

"What are you talking about?" I asked.

"Guys, it's possible we are about to ride into our destiny."

The three of us stared down that narrow country road. I started my Husky. Charles started his Eagle. I looked at him. He was smiling. I looked back at Gary. So was he. And away we went.

A minute later, we crossed the bridge and turned onto the trail that led to the river. Now we were looking everywhere for *The Thing*. We reached the river safely enough and parked our scooters and left them running. When we reached the top of the bank and looked down, a chill went up our spines. Our gear and food were scattered everywhere. We looked at each other, then around us in every direction. We listened. Nothing. Charles started down the bank, and Gary and I followed. No one said a word as we gathered our stuff and climbed back up. We tied it to our scooters the best we could, and then Charles started back down the bank.

"Where are you *going?* I asked nervously.

"To look at the trap. I want to know."

I looked at Gary and started back down to join him. Gary followed, too. No way was he staying behind all alone. We reached the trap—rather, where the trap had been. *It was gone*. There remained only the steel stake we had driven into the ground and one-half of the first link of the steel chain. We didn't bother to retrieve it. In record time, we were back on our scooters and outta there.

Back in town, we dropped our things off and returned to Joe's. We sat in our favorite booth near the jukebox. Joe walked over.

"Hi, men," he said. "Let me guess: three Cokes—one vanilla, one cherry, and one chocolate." We nodded.

Gary went to the jukebox. He returned just as Joe brought our Cokes.

"Guys, if I didn't know better, I'd say you three had just seen a ghost." We smiled, and he went back to the kitchen. Behind us, from the jukebox, in rich, full, stereophonic sound, the Troggs launched into their number one hit, "Wild Thing."

We both looked at Gary. Charles said it before I could. "What are you, some kind of comedian?"

We sat there, laughing, drinking our Cokes, and listening to the music, while somewhere out there, something lurked.

Chapter 26

WE DECIDED to sit on the Bigfoot story for a while. It's a good thing we did. The next week, the *Archer County News* ran a front-page photograph of Mac Baugh sitting on his tractor and pointing to the spot where he had sighted the "Creature." In the article he described how he was out plowing when "it just came out of the brush and walked right across my field, like nobody's business." He described it as "eight or nine feet tall, and looked like nothin' I've ever seen in these parts before." The article was the talk of the town, and Mac was taking quite a ribbing. The question on most folks' minds was, was he sober at the time? He was known to have a beer or two from time to time—even when plowing. Evidently, one morning some years back, he climbed aboard his Ford tractor with a full cooler and set about cultivating his ten acres. When finished, he'd plowed approximately one-third of Archer County—or so the story goes. Still, the fact that someone else had seen something was on our minds. And plenty scary.

Tonight, though, it was me that was taking a beating. Charles had stolen Raylette's car again, and we had been to Wichita, where the three of us had almost managed to completely exhaust the city's supply of Pizza Hut pizza. Then we had gone to a movie. I somehow managed to convince them to see *The Sound of Music*. I had seen it already and loved it. But to put it mildly, Charles and Gary weren't big on it.

"I can't *believe* we just saw that," Charles was saying as we drove home. "A musical. A *three-hour musical,* for crying out loud. I swear, if anybody finds out, I'll never forgive you, Bubba."

"It wasn't *that* bad," I was saying. "What'd you think, Gary?"

"I say if anyone asks, we just say we went to see *The Good, the Bad and the Ugly*, which is where we should have gone in the first place. How could we have passed up Clint Eastwood for a bunch of singing nuns? I'm embarrassed just thinking about it."

"Bubba, you owe us, big time. And I ain't gonna forget it, either."

"Me neither," Gary added. "And from now on, Charles and I pick the movies. You're outta the loop."

"You got *that* right," Charles said. "Bubba, you need help."

"Okay," I said. "Just let me out here, and I'll walk."

"You're not gettin' off *that* easy." He smiled.

We were almost to the river, and despite their threats and badgering, I felt good. It was raining. Raining hard. Back to the west was some serious lightning—more rain on the way. If this kept up, the river would be running again before long. I couldn't wait. Then we crossed the river bridge, and I saw something that stopped my heart.

"Pull over!" I shouted.

"What?"

"Pull over! Now!"

Charles looked over at me and pulled onto the shoulder. As soon as we stopped, I jumped out and ran back toward the bridge. I could hear them yelling at me.

"Where the hell are you going? What is it?"

I ran. Behind me, I could hear Charles backing up. When I got to the spot, I saw what I was afraid I'd seen. It was Tick the Dog.

He was lying just off the shoulder. He'd been run over. The

car was right behind me now, and the backup lights lit the scene. Charles set the brake and they got out. It was pouring rain.

"What is it?" Gary asked.

"It's Tick the Dog," I said. "Sam's dog. The one I told you about. I think he's hurt bad. We've got to get him home."

"Well, let's put him in the car and get going," Charles said.

"Can't," I answered. "There's no road to Sam's—only a trail. We'll have to walk."

"In the dark? In the rain? Along the river?" Gary was asking nervously.

We all looked at each other. He was right. For a moment, no one spoke.

Then Charles said, "The hell with it. I've got a flashlight in the car. Let's do it."

He went after it and killed the engine. I reached down to pick up Tick. I knew he was hurt and scared. He growled for a second when I reached under him—but just once.

The walk to Sam's was a tough one. Besides being dark (the flashlight lasted about five minutes before the bulb burned out), the trail was muddy and slick. It continued to rain hard. We were soaked and Tick was heavy. Finally, we saw the lights. When we were about a hundred yards from the house, Sam saw us. He had been sitting outside on the porch. He hurried to us.

He looked at Tick, then at the three of us. He took him from Gary's arms. The dog whimpered and looked up at him. Their eyes met. I wondered what they were thinking.

"We took turns carrying him, Sam."

He looked up at me. "Would you boys please come up to the house for a moment?" he asked.

"Sure," I answered.

He turned, and we followed him. When we reached the

porch, Rose was there waiting on us. We stepped up out of the rain.

"Rose, darlin', Jim and his buddies here have brought this old mutt back to us. I guess we're just never gonna get rid of him." He sat down in the rocker with the dog in his arms.

Rose placed a hand on his shoulder. Fighting back tears, she said, "Jim, I've not had the honor of meeting your friends here."

I introduced them.

"Sam and I can only hope that someday you boys will know what you've done for us. And what this means to us. That will be our prayer."

There was a flash of lightning, and then thunder.

"Would you boys like to come in and dry off?" she asked.

"No ma'am," I said. "It doesn't look like it's going to let up. We better head back."

"Please be careful," she said.

The three of us said goodbye and left. After we'd gone a ways, I turned and glanced back. Rose had pulled a chair over next to Sam and was sitting, rubbing his back, trying to console him. Sam appeared to be bent over, talking in Tick's ear.

When we finally reached the car, we were exhausted. We climbed in and just sat there, glad to be out of the rain.

"Thanks, guys," I said. "I owe you. I won't ever tell anyone what you did if you don't want me to."

"You better not," Charles said. "I don't want anyone to know about this." He looked over at Gary and winked. " 'Cause if anyone ever finds out that we went to see a three-hour musical about a bunch of nuns, my reputation is ruined."

And they laughed. It took me a second to catch on. Then I laughed, too. And we sat there, all soaking wet, on the side of the road, and it felt good. We probably should have been worried about all the mud in Raylette's car. But we weren't.

Chapter 27

TICK THE DOG died that night, shortly after we left. I arrived at Sam's the next day just as he finished burying him. Rose was sitting on the porch rocking when I walked up.

"Samuel's around back," she said to me. "You go right on back there. He'll be glad to see you."

I nodded and headed that way.

"Jim," Rose called after me. I stopped.

"He thinks the world of you."

I didn't know what to say. I looked at her, hesitated, then continued on. Sam was leaning on a shovel by the grave, looking not at it, but far away. I walked up beside him.

"You okay?" I asked.

"Sure," he answered softly. "Water's a bit rough right now, but it'll pass. Always does."

He looked at me and managed a smile. "You have a dog?" he asked.

"Used to," I said. A cocker spaniel. His name was Skipper. He died last year."

"That's a shame," he said.

"Someone poisoned him," I said. "For a long time, I thought it was Harley. I don't anymore."

"What made you think that?"

"Well, one evening he walked by our house, and after he'd gone past, I began to throw rocks at him. I didn't hit him, he was too far away, but I came pretty close."

"Why did you do that?"

"I don't know. I just thought he was weird—him walking at night and all. And I had heard he was a window peeker. But what's crazy, is the whole time I was throwing those rocks, I felt terrible for doing it. He never looked back. Just kept walking. Anyway, the next day when I got home from school, Skipper was real sick. Mom and I took him in the kitchen so he could lay on the cool linoleum floor, but he started having convulsions and couldn't get up. After a while, he died. And later, when Mom went to get his water bowl, she found ground glass in it. I just assumed Harley did it."

"And now you don't?" he asked.

"No. I don't," I said.

He smiled, looked away again, and said, "You hear that?"

"What?"

"That little river is runnin' like there's no tomorrow. Let's go fishin'."

I smiled. "That sounds like a good idea."

When we got back around front, Sam's fishing gear was on the porch. He looked over at me and smiled.

Rose stuck her head out the screen door, wiping her hands on her apron. "I want you to know I got my heart set on fresh catfish for supper, now, you hear?"

"Well, you best be gettin' the grease hot, 'cause it won't be long," Sam told her. Sam and I waved goodbye and headed down the trail.

The trail was still muddy from the night before, but the rain had cooled things off some. It wasn't long before we were there.

We had to sit high on the bank—the river was really up. I sat watching the muddy water, thinking. I looked over at Sam.

"What did you mean back there when you said, 'Water's a bit rough right now, but it'll pass'?"

He looked over but didn't say anything.

"Were you talking about this river?"

"No, son. Not this little ol' river. I was referrin' to the River Big."

"Where's that?"

He smiled. And chuckled. "Well, now, I 'spect you're just about sittin' smack-dab in the middle of it."

I stared at him. Waiting.

"You see, it has just always felt to me like we're all floatin' in a big river . . . and the current's carryin' us along . . . some parts flowin' slow and easy—that's when times are good; and some parts are pretty rough—bad times for sure.

"The way I see it, we're all just sort of born into it, and after that, we're on our own. What I haven't figured out is why some folks seem to spend most their lives in the rough water. I been there, that's for sure. And I reckon there *are* times when the current's just too strong to escape. But sometimes, I think you *can* swim out of it, if you want to bad enough and try hard enough. Sometimes. And I believe we're put here for a reason. And we're supposed to find that reason somewhere along the way. I ain't sure yet just what it is, but I'll know it when I see it one of these days." He paused, and then looked over at me. "Now, why would you let a fool old man ramble on like that?"

"What does Rose think about all that?"

He smiled. "She says I'm leavin' the Lord out."

"Sounds like you are."

"Not really. I reckon He drops us in at the beginning. And at the end, pulls us out and judges how we done."

"Yeah, but does He stay out of it? Or does He get involved?"

"Rose would say He most definitely has a hand in it— because how else can you account for miracles?"

"What do *you* think?" I wanted to know.

"I don't know, son. That does tend to complicate things a mite, don't it?"

"Yeah," I said. "It does."

We sat there, lost in our thoughts. In the distance, a truck labored down the highway. He seemed a world away. But he wasn't. Sam was right—we're all in this together.

Part Three

LATE SUMMER

Chapter 28

IN MY DREAM, *there were flowers everywhere. As far as I could see. Every kind imaginable. I wandered about, felt a little lost, but not the least bit scared. Rather, I had a peaceful, easy feeling. Then I heard a voice.*

"Welcome," it said.

I turned and saw someone walking toward me.

It was Sam.

"Where are we?" I asked.

"A very special place," he said, smiling.

"Which way is town?" I asked, trying to get my bearings.

He laughed. "Well, now, I don't rightly know. Besides, that don't matter right now. What matters is that you found your way here."

I looked around. "What's with all these flowers? Where'd they come from?"

He smiled again and said, "Son, this is the Garden of Hearts. The most extraordinary of gardens."

"Garden of Hearts?"

"Yes. You see, all of these flowers have a special meaning. Each one stands for a person in your life—all the people who care about you, and all the people you've met."

"I don't get it," I said.

"I know you don't. But don't be concerned with how or why. That's not important."

I stood there trying to take it all in. There were flowers of all shapes and sizes and all colors. "So you're saying these represent people I know?" I asked.

"That's right," he answered.

"And each one belongs to a different person?"

He nodded. "And somethin' else," he said. "Each flower's beauty shows how that person feels about you."

I looked at the ones directly at my feet. They were small and pink and white in color. Periwinkles, I think. Next to them were some violets. I looked around. There were marigolds, and coneflowers. Daylilies and roses. And more.

"Some of these must mean someone cares for me an awful lot."

"That they do," he replied.

"Do you know who each flower belongs to?"

"As a matter of fact, I do." He smiled.

"Then all I have to do is pick them out and ask you whose they are?"

"Not exactly, son. As I said, this is a special place, and it has special rules. You can only ask about one flower. That's all."

"I see," I said. "Is there anything else?"

"Yes. One thing more. You can never come back here."

I stood there wondering how this could be happening. But it was. The flowers were real. They were alive and their scents filled the air. I looked at Sam. "I've decided," I said.

"I know," he replied. "There's only one flower out here you want to see."

"How do you know that?"

"That's why we're here. There's a flower here I wanted you to see. One you deserve to see. Hers is down this way, son."

I followed him a short ways and he stopped and looked at me. I looked down at the flower before us. It was small and sort of yellow in color. It had barely begun to bloom.

"Are you sure this is the right one?" I asked.

"Yes, son," he answered. "It's Lorrie's."

It was pretty, but I was disappointed. Sam sensed my disappointment and put his hand on my shoulder.

"Son, you have no idea how lucky you are."

"I don't understand."

"I know you don't," he said, "but you see, son, what you have here is a golden orchid—the rarest and most beautiful flower of them all. It just hasn't fully bloomed yet."

"What are you saying?"

"Unlike the others, this flower stands for much more than just how she feels about you. It's the reason I brought you here—so you'd know."

He paused for a moment and then continued. "Son, I believe that for every person on this earth there is one other—and that those two were meant to be together. However, most never find each other. And the reason is simple. Most never cross paths. They may live oceans apart, and that's sad. Or they may live their whole lives just miles apart, yet never meet. And that's sadder still. But, son, sometimes by chance, or by God's doin', they do find each other. And when that happens, somethin' very special happens. Maybe not right away, but in time. I know. It happened to me. Mine was a rose. And yours is this golden orchid."

I stood staring at the flower, and I knew Sam was right. I'd known it when I first laid eyes on her. I hadn't been able to put it into words. Now Sam had done that.

When I looked up, he was gone.

The sun was going down, and it would be dark soon. I took one last long look at the orchid and turned to leave. I wasn't sure which way to go, so I just walked. Soon I emerged from the flowers and found the river before me. I stopped and looked back. The garden was gone. There remained only a small *clearing—in it just a few rocks and some weeds. I walked west along the river toward the setting sun. When I reached our fishing spot, I saw Sam sitting on the bank on the other side. He was by himself. What was he doing there? I wondered. The river was dry as a bone. And he looked so alone. Tick the Dog should have been there. But he wasn't. No one was. Finally, he got up and turned and climbed the bank. I called out to him. He paused at the top, his back to me. He didn't hear me. I yelled again. But he walked away. And soon he was gone.*

I awoke.

Chapter 29

As I pulled into Benny's Fina that afternoon, Charles was getting a Coke out of the machine, and Gary was airing up some kid's bicycle tire. I parked next to Charles's scooter and got off. I'd decided against telling them about my dream. At least for now. Gary walked past, and we followed him into the grease stall. He had called an emergency meeting, and he looked pretty serious. Something was up.

"Either of you seen the Archer paper?"

We looked at each other and shook our heads.

He pulled one out of his back pocket and spread it on the workbench.

Creature captured, the headlines read. We looked up at him.

"Yeah, it turns out Bigfoot is an ostrich. What we saw that night was an *ostrich*." he said.

"No way. No friggin' way." Charles wasn't buying it. Neither was I.

"Oh, it was an ostrich, all right. It escaped from its cage when a travelin' circus stopped south of town a while back. They even offered a reward. And two days ago, it wandered into Katy Poole's backyard. The article says it was attracted by the smell of fish hangin' from her clothesline." Charles and I looked at each other.

"That couldn't have been an ostrich we saw that night," I said.

"Keep reading. There was a small steel trap dangling from

one foot when they found it. Now, where do you suppose she got that?"

"She?"

"Yeah. *She*. As if this wasn't bad enough, it's a girl. Her name is Minnie Mae, for crying out loud. Can you believe it? What you guys were running from that night was just a big bird. A girl one, at that."

"What do you mean, *you guys?*" Charles wanted to know.

"I was only running because y'all were. What we should have done was catch the darn thing. Then we'd have gotten the reward and our picture in the paper."

I looked at the photo. It showed Minnie Mae flanked by Katy, Mac Baugh, and the smiling circus owner. It seems Katy got the reward, Mac took some more ribbing because of his reported "sighting," and the ostrich headed back to the circus.

We all looked at each other.

"Well, I know one thing," Charles said. "It's a darn good thing we didn't tell anyone, or we'd never have lived it down."

"No kidding," I added.

"It's still humiliating," Gary said.

"Yeah. It is *that*," I agreed.

"We've got to do something to bounce back. Our morale needs it. You guys agree?"

"Yeah. But what?"

"Something big." Gary was smiling. "And I've got it covered. Follow me."

We followed him out the backdoor to a small storage building. He unlocked it, and we stepped in. It was dark, hot, and dusty. There was junk piled everywhere. Most of it had clearly been there for years. Gary walked over, pulled a small cardboard carton out from beneath a cabinet, and set it on the floor at our feet. He opened it and looked up at us.

"Is that what I think it is?" Charles asked.

Gary nodded.

"What?" I asked.

Charles looked at me, then back down. "Gunpowder."

"*What?* Where'd you get *that?*" I wanted to know.

"Benny got it somewhere. I think some guy traded it to him for a tire."

"What's Benny gonna do with it?" I asked.

"Nothin' now. Probably forgot it's even here."

"What are *we* gonna do with it?" I asked.

"We're gonna light up this town. You ready for this? The World's Greatest Bottle Rocket!"

"Cool!" Charles exclaimed.

"What are you hooligans up to?" a voice shouted from behind us. We jumped a foot in the air and turned, expecting the worst.

"Plannin' on robbin' a bank, or just blowin' up the town?" It was Roy. Jesse was looking over his shoulder.

We all caught our breath. Gary answered. "No, we're just going to make a little rocket."

Roy eyed us closely and smiled. "Aspirin bottle works best. You just screw off the top, fill it up with powder, and put the lid back on real tight, leavin' a little hole in it for the fuse. But be sure you punch the hole before you put the lid back on. Otherwise that one little spark could cause you a heapful of trouble."

We three smiled at each other. "Anything else?"

"Yeah. Make sure the fuse is plenty long."

Jesse snickered from behind.

"You guys aren't going to say anything about this to anyone, are you?" Gary asked nervously.

Roy smiled, showing his tobacco-stained teeth. He shook

his head. "Naw," he said. He turned and pushed Jesse out the door. "Come on. Let's go 'fore they blow this place up!"

We watched them leave, closed the door behind them, and looked at each other.

"All right! Let's get this show on the road!"

Chapter 30

LAUNCH SITE. Eleven P.M. The baseball diamond. Second base.

T-minus-one minute and counting. We three stand staring at our creation. A six-inch-long Bayer aspirin bottle carefully packed full of gunpowder and taped to the end of a twenty-four-inch piece of balsa wood with a twelve-inch fuse made from kite string soaked in lighter fluid. Perched ready and waiting and aimed precisely at the Big Dipper.

T-minus-thirty seconds and counting. We shake hands, and Charles hands me his Bic lighter. Then he and Gary turn and run toward right field. Having won the coin toss, I have the dubious honor of launching our creation.

T-minus-fifteen seconds and counting. I bend down in the dark and flick the Bic. Everything looks good.

T-minus-five seconds. It's a go. I light the fuse.

It's at that moment that I became fully aware of the power of the human brain and what it is really capable of. I would never have dreamed it possible to have one hundred thoughts simultaneously, but it is. I was having them. And ninety were saying the same thing: *Runnnnnnnn!*

At the rate the flame was racing up the fuse, one of those

thoughts told me the fuse needed to be about twelve feet in length. Not twelve inches. Another said I was about to have all sorts of questions answered about rocket propulsion and the afterlife. Finally, one did take charge and sent the necessary information and electrical impulses to my legs so that I could get up and run like crazy. I did. I managed to go five steps before the night lit up like a camera flash. There was a really loud boom, and someone or something kicked me in the back and sent me sprawling face first into the dirt and stickers.

I lay there motionless while a choir somewhere played "Alleluia" in my ears with handbells. Shortly, they finished, and the next voice I heard was that of God. Or Charles. I wasn't sure.

"You all right?"

I opened my eyes and saw a pair of penny loafers. A good sign.

"Are my legs still attached?" I asked nervously.

"Yeah. Don't those stickers hurt?"

"Yes, as a matter of fact, they do," I replied.

"Want some help getting up?"

"That would be nice."

They each grabbed an arm and helped me up. We spent the next few minutes pulling goathead stickers from the front half of my anatomy. I think the big one on the end of my nose hurt the most. I'm not sure. We had barely finished when Gary gasped.

"Holy cow! Would you look at that?" He was staring at the launch site. Or what remained of it.

Before us was a crater about ten feet in diameter and a couple of feet deep. Needless to say, second base was nowhere to be found. We looked at each other.

"We better scram!" I can't recall who made that suggestion, but we all agreed it was in our best interest. We ran like hell. After we jumped the outfield fence (it was only two feet high), Gary stopped to suck on his inhaler. His eyes suddenly grew to the size of quarters. "Oh my gosh, look!"

There, hovering just off the ground near the middle of the infield, was a perfectly shaped mushroom cloud of smoke. We ran approximately half a mile before I had to stop again.

"Hang on, guys. We must have missed some stickers." I reached into my jeans and rubbed my rear end.

"You didn't have any on your backside, Bubba," Charles reminded me.

My hand was wet. I pulled it out and looked. It was covered with blood. I reached back down and felt again. Suddenly I knew where most of the aspirin bottle had wound up. "I think I'm hurt, guys," I said, showing them the blood.

"Can you walk?" Gary asked.

"I think so. Let's head to my house. It's closest."

They walked me home. We stayed clear of the streetlights and hid from any cars that we met. We managed to make it before long.

Mom was watching TV as we entered and walked past her toward my bedroom. She looked up. "Everything all right?" she asked.

We all nodded.

"You boys look like you're up to something."

"Naw, we're just going to listen to some records."

She smiled. "Okay. By the way, there's Cokes in the fridge if you want them."

"Thanks," I said. We then hurried into the bedroom.

Once inside, I pulled off my jeans and my blood-soaked underwear. I didn't know whether to laugh or cry.

They took one look and knew what had to be done. Charles put a Beatles record on and turned it up so she couldn't hear, and Gary went to get some tweezers. He returned shortly with a pair. And three Cokes, and a bag of Fritos.

"What did she say?" I asked.

"She asked if I was hungry."

"No, I mean about the tweezers."

"Oh. Nothing. I just told her you had a splinter."

An hour later, all visible fragments of glass had carefully been removed from my lower torso. Gary was given the duty of smuggling my red underpants out and discarding them. He was not happy about it, but after all, this whole thing had been his idea in the first place. *The World's Greatest Bottle Rocket. Right.*

Chapter 31

"My dad was an athlete, too, you know," I said.

Sam looked over. "Is that so?"

I nodded. Sam was wearing an old wide-brimmed straw hat that made him look kind of silly. I couldn't say much, though, because the truth is, I'd have liked to have had it. The hot August sun was fierce, and the top of my head was hot as a firecracker.

"He played football."

"You don't say. That's a good sport, too," he answered as he reeled in his line to check his bait.

"Yeah. Uncle Pyle said Jacksboro High School only lost three games in the three years my dad played quarterback there. And even though Jacksboro's only a little bigger than Archer City, there's been two college All-Americans come from there. He said Daddy could've been the third if he'd only had the chance."

"Did he get hurt?"

"No. Nothing like that." I paused. "When he graduated, the coach at Texas A&M wanted him to come play there. He wanted to. But his mom, my Grandma Ida, was against it. So instead he went to a little college just across the Louisiana border. But he only stayed there one semester."

Sam waited for me to continue.

"Uncle Pyle said he knew it would happen. He said Grandma Ida phoned Daddy every week begging him to come home. Wanted to know why he'd abandoned her."

"That's too bad," Sam said. I could tell he meant it.

"Anyway, he came back and enrolled at Decatur Baptist College only fifty miles away. But it was the same as before. And he just couldn't stand to listen to her cry. Uncle Pyle said it was a pattern he knew well. It was about that time Daddy started drinking, he said."

"How'd your granddaddy feel 'bout all this?" he asked.

"He wasn't alive. He died when Daddy was about eight. And the weird thing is, Grandma Ida never told them why he died. Uncle Pyle said during his last few days, there was always someone sitting with him by his bed—either people from church or the Odd Fellows Lodge. Then one night he and Daddy woke up and could hear Grandma Ida screaming and crying, and they knew he'd died. But it was years later before they found out why." I looked at Sam. "Ain't that something?"

I found myself wishing Tick the Dog was still around so I could pet him. He was good at knowing when people were sad. I felt a tug on my fishing line but paid it no mind. I wanted to finish what I'd started.

"I think maybe that's why he liked baseball so much, later on. That thinking about football made him sad."

"Could be, son. I can see how that might happen. But it might be he don't care 'bout that anymore."

I looked up. "What do you mean?"

"Well, my granddaddy used to say the hereafter is like a piece of glass you can only see through on one side. He called it death's mirror. We can't see the dead. But he believed they can see us. *That they can look back.* If that's so, I 'spect your daddy is proud of what he sees and don't think much about that other anymore."

"You think they can do that? Look back?"

"I don't know. I reckon maybe. I guess we'll have to wait to find out."

I looked out at the river. "You know, sometimes I wonder how things would be today if Daddy *had* gone to college and played football."

Sam looked over. "You might not even be sittin' here, had that happened," he said.

He was right. We probably never would have moved to Archer City. And I'd never have met Sam. Or Charles or Gary. Lorrie. What would I do if I could choose now? It had only been four years since he died, and already I had trouble remembering his face. His voice. What if I could choose? What if I *had* to?

Sam clearly noticed. "Don't fret over it, son," he said. "You'll worry yourself sick. I know. It's been my experience that there's not much we can do about the past—no matter how much we want to change it."

He was right. I guess I already knew that, but I needed to hear it. I needed to be reminded. I think most people do.

Chapter 32

OKAY, HERE'S WHERE LOVE fits into Sam's River Big scheme: in the rapids, that's where. Turbulent water. To be fair, there should be a sign posted saying: WARNING—YOU ARE ENTER-ING DANGEROUS TERRITORY.

The ball game in Windthorst I'd been waiting anxiously for had finally arrived. I'd made sure Mom washed and *ironed* my uniform. Even Charles and Gary were on hand. It was dur-ing warm-ups that I spotted her—the prettiest brown eyes I had ever seen. *Sitting next to a cowboy*. I couldn't believe it. A danged old cowboy. I'm sorry. But I just never cared for them. And I sure didn't like this one. He was at least a couple of years older than me. He had on *starched* jeans and a shirt with sharp creases. A cowboy hat *way* too big for his head. A *dip* of tobacco under his lip. And *cowshit* on his boots. Or horseshit. Some kind of shit. I was devastated. When she looked in my direction, I had to look away. I thought about the Garden of Hearts, and the orchid, and everything Sam had said in the dream. If she only knew. But she didn't. What a waste. What a dadgum waste.

The game started, and for the first few innings I was useless. Boy, was I down. Then, gradually, I began to get my second wind. By the fifth inning, I had pretty much put it behind me. Not only that, I had an idea. I'd show her. I'd show them all. You can't keep a good man down. As we took the field, I ran over to Coach Mike.

"Coach, I want to pitch." He looked at me like I was crazy.

"No, I'm serious. Let me pitch. You owe it to me."

"How's that?"

"Because I took two in the ribs for you earlier in the season when no one else would, that's why. And I'm just now fully recovering from those. So, please. What do you say? The game isn't even that close, and besides, we've got a good lead."

He look around.

"Please."

The umpire had walked over. "Let's go, Coach. You need one more player."

Coach Mike nodded to the ump and then faced me. "All right. You win. You go to the mound and send Eddie to the outfield."

"Thanks! You won't regret it!" And I sprinted to the pitcher's mound. Eddie didn't believe me, so Coach Mike had to motion him to center field. He dropped the ball in my glove and left.

The announcer made the announcement. "There's been a change for Archer City . . . Now pitching . . . Jim Black." Gary and Charles cheered and whistled. I think there was some applause, but I'm not sure. I know there was a lot of murmuring in the crowd. I took my warm-up tosses and signaled I was ready. The umpire said, "Play ball!" And the batter stepped in.

When I saw who it was, I realized I should have paid closer attention when I chose to ask to pitch. Then it came: "Now batting for Windthorst . . . 'Jackhammer' Schroeder." No one called Jackhammer by his real first name. He preferred it that way, and if you saw him, you wouldn't argue. He was fifteen going on thirty, with arms the size of his legs. That was the bad news. The good news was, being a Schroeder, he was most likely Lorrie's cousin somewhere down the line. Perfect. I didn't bother to look into the stands. I knew her eyes were on me. Everyone's were. What they didn't know was I had an advantage. A secret weapon . . . the infamous knuckle curveball! Now, Sam hadn't actually taught it to me, but I had watched him use it plenty. And I had a pretty good idea how to throw it. Redemption time was here.

I stared in at the catcher, nodded at his first sign so Jackhammer would think fastball, and took a glance over at the runner on first. Then I took my stretch, raised the ball to my lips, kissed it, rocked back, made a high leg kick, let it go, and smiled.

It reached the plate in a graceful arch, but failed to drop. Or curve. Or do anything. Jackhammer's eyes grew wide as he watched it come in, and at the last instant, he swung with all his might. There was a loud pop, and everyone watched it disappear into the night air, followed by a strange whistling sound. Moments later, there was the distinct sound of glass breaking when it reached the gymnasium far in the distance. No one moved or made a sound. The stadium was deathly quiet. Jackhammer rounded the bases in total silence, occasionally sneaking glances in the direction of the school and shaking his head. I walked over and took a seat on the bench. Coach Mike never even noticed me. Like everyone else, he simply stood, staring spellbound into the dark beyond the outfield fence.

Chapter 33

I ESCAPED TO THE SAFETY of the water tower the next night. But not alone. Charles and Gary had come to make sure I didn't jump. It was cool up high, and the sounds below and in the distance were soft and comforting. Now if I could just get the two of them to stop talking about it.

"I didn't think it was possible for a human being to hit a ball that far," Gary was saying.

"Me neither," Charles answered.

"Hey, you might get in the *Guinness Book of World Records!*"

"I was just the pitcher, remember?" I said, trying to muster some sarcasm.

"Maybe they'll put you both in there. They ought to."

"Can we just drop it?" I pleaded.

"Yeah. You're right," Charles said. "You've been through a lot. Lost your girl *and* suffered public humiliation in the same night. However, I'm guessing if you'd left well enough alone, you could've stopped with the first and prevented the second."

"Yeah," Gary said, "but if you're gonna go down, you might as well go down in flames."

"Thanks a lot. You guys are great."

They laughed.

"Hey, it could've been worse, you know." Gary was on a roll.

"How's that?"

"He could've hit a line drive and killed you."

They died laughing.

Then, "You know what this means, don't you?" Charles asked.

"No, what?"

"Porky's probably gonna go after her."

He might. Just two years earlier he'd gone after Karen Holder. It wasn't five minutes after she had broken up with me, he was asking her to go with him. However, I didn't let that come between our friendship. (Her answer, I recall, wasn't just no, but *heck no!* That may have had something to do with it.)

"Naw," Gary was saying. "She's not my type. And until I get me some wheels, I better stick to the girls here in Archer."

Charles laughed, and looked over at Heathcliff, and nudged him. "What do you think about it?"

Heathcliff didn't answer. Rather, he stared blankly into space. It was no wonder. This homemade dummy had been through a lot. He'd been run over, dragged behind a car, shot at, and hunted by the law.

"What did you bring him up here for?" I asked.

" 'Cause he's better company than you right now."

I managed a smile and looked at Heathcliff. I noticed one of his eyes was falling out. Charles noticed it, too, and pushed it back in.

"He needs an overhaul. He's plumb fallin' apart."

Little did we know that tonight would be his final curtain call.

"It's getting late, are y'all ready?" Charles asked.

"Yeah, I don't think I could take much more of you cheering me up, anyway," I said.

We laughed. Then Charles hoisted Heathcliff over the rail and held him while Gary secured him around the waist with rope. We were pretty sure that, from the ground, he would appear to be some man hanging on for dear life. When he finished, we climbed down.

Once we were a few hundred feet away, we turned and looked. It was so dark, we could hardly see him. No one was likely to even notice him.

"Dang. Think we oughta take him down?" Gary asked.

"Naw," Charles answered. "Let's just leave him there. I'm tired."

"Me, too. Let's call it a night."

And we did.

My phone rang at 6:45 the next morning. It was Gary.

"We're in trouble. We might have messed up this time."

"Why? What happened?"

"Heathcliff."

"What about him?"

"Well, sometime in the night, the wind blew him loose. Only he didn't fall. This morning, from the ground, he looks like some guy who hung himself last night."

"You're kidding."

"Nope. I wish I was. Mrs. Olsen spotted him when she went out to get her paper. Went screaming into the house and called the sheriff. Well, he gets there, and he's certain it's a suicide, so he calls the fire department to get him down."

"You've *got* to be kidding."

"Nope. It gets worse. They get there, and Alvin climbs up to where he's hanging, sees it's a dummy, takes out his knife, and cuts the rope. Well, the people on the ground don't know it's a dummy. So when he hits the ground, Mrs. Olsen faints dead away."

"Is she okay?"

"I don't know. They took her in the ambulance. You suppose they can get us for murder?"

"No! I don't think so. Where's Charles?"

"He'd already heard about it when I called him. Said he was gonna get outta Dodge for a while. I think he went to Wichita."

"Well, let's just lay low and see what happens. Be sure and keep me posted."

"Will do," Gary said. "But if we do go to prison, can I bunk with you?"

"Will you stop that? We're not going anywhere," I told him, then I hung up.

At least I hoped not.

Chapter 34

THIS WASN'T LIKE SAM. He never missed fishing on Saturdays. I laid my gear on the ground and headed for his house.

A week had gone by since the hanging, and things had pretty much cooled off. It turns out Mrs. Olsen hadn't fainted at all. Just got caught up in the excitement and liked all the attention. The *Archer County News* failed to get there in time for a photo, and asked that someone climb back up and reattach Heathcliff. No one did. We were never even questioned about it, although Sheriff Harris did give us the once-over in Joe's a few days later. I guess you could say things were back to normal. Except for Sam.

As I reached his house, I spotted him sitting on the edge of the front porch. I walked up and sat beside him. He had been doodling in the dirt with a stick.

"Everything okay?" I asked, a little anxiously.

He shook his head.

"What's wrong?" I was suddenly worried.

"Harold," he replied.

"What happened?"

"Some boys, or men, I don't know . . . someone . . ." He grew quiet.

"What? What is it?"

"They found him, some hunters did, yesterday, out near Chalk Hill. He was blindfolded and had his hands tied behind his back. Someone had dumped him out there like that and left him. Them fellers that found him said it looked like he'd been out there for days. He was pretty scratched up and filthy. And scared plumb to death." He looked away.

"I don't know, son. I just don't know anymore. Why would someone do a thing like that? And where does a person go to get away from it? I just don't know where to go."

He paused. "Rose, she's back there in the bedroom right now readin' her Bible, bless her heart. I told her I don't think the answer's in there, but she says it's all we have." He looked over at me. "What do you think, son?"

"I don't know," I answered. "I was hoping you'd tell *me*."

He turned and looked out at the river. "The men that found him didn't know what to do with him, seein' as how he wouldn't talk to 'em. So they took him to the sheriff's office. Sheriff Harris wanted to take him to the hospital, but he wouldn't go. So he took him home and came out here and told me about it. He was nice enough to take me to see him, but when we got there, Harold wouldn't open the door. Wouldn't even talk to me. I don't know if he'll ever come out."

Shortly, I left Sam's. I stopped at the river, got my fishing stuff, and went straight home. Once there, I gathered up some food in a sack. Beans, soup, bread, and leftover pie. And Coke. And I drove to Harley's home.

The sun was going down, and the tiny house was dark. I knocked and got no answer. I didn't want to upset him, so I placed the items next to his door and left. The following day I drove past and saw they were still sitting there. The next day they were gone.

It was a couple of weeks before he came out. When he did, he was different. He began walking during the day some and held his head just slightly higher so he could see around him a little better. And rather than carry his hands at his sides, his right one was always in his trouser pocket. Some speculated he had a knife in the pocket. Or a razor. But someone said it was a rabbit's foot. And I believed them. Meanwhile, Sheriff Harris put the word out that if he ever found out whose sick idea of a joke that was, he would prosecute them to the full extent of the law. And then he'd deal with them personally. He visited Harley often and assured him nothing like that would ever happen again. Not in his county.

I asked around and discovered he and Harley had been good friends growing up. Pals. And something else. Harley's real name was Harold Horton. Some remembered him as a bright kid in school and a nice young man who loved motor-cycles. Normal in every way. Until the accident. If all of this was true, then he must have had other friends back then, besides the sheriff. I wondered where they were now. And his parents. Most thought they moved away shortly after he graduated from high school, and no one could remember them ever returning to see about him after he got hurt.

I spotted him one day sitting on his front porch shelling peas. I waved when I went past, and he waved back. I would only see Harley once more that summer. And although I didn't know it at the time, that would be the last time anyone would see him alive.

Chapter 35

WE SAT IN THE ROYAL THEATER not moving or making a sound. Charles said I'd been way too quiet lately thinking about too many things, but that this would get my mind off them. He was right. I was concentrating only on the bottom of the screen. Focused on a spot low enough that I could only detect movement above, not discern what it was. I didn't know if Charles was watching or not. I noticed Gary had his jacket over his head and one sleeve held up. I waved my hand back and forth in front of it with no response. I punched him.

"Don't act like you're watching!" I said.

"I am!"

"I know durn well you're not. I—"

"You guys are missing this," Charles interrupted. "She's takin' off her clothes."

We both looked up to see a close-up of the man with the burned-up head and face with no eyes. Gary screamed.

"Dang it, Charles!" I said. "Quit it!"

He laughed, then suddenly grew quiet, his eyes wide. I looked down.

It wasn't bad enough that the guy on-screen looked the way he did, but to make things worse, he was bent on revenge. We thought Barbara Stanwyck had done him in earlier in the movie, but she hadn't. We sure wished she had. Now he was always suddenly appearing from behind doors and trees—usually in thick smoke or fog. We had seen some lulus before, but this one took the cake. Soon as it was over, we hightailed it out of there. Outside, we stopped only long enough to look up at the marquee, which warned: NIGHT WALKER.

I insisted we walk to my house together. After all, there was strength in numbers. I got no argument from them. We walked right down the very middle of the road the whole way, convinced the guy from the movie was following alongside us just out of sight. We finally made it to my house. Mom and I drove Charles and Gary home, and morning couldn't come soon enough.

The next afternoon I was asleep on the couch because I'd gotten no sleep the night before. I heard a honk and jumped, still a little skittish. Through our picture window I saw Charles's granddad's pickup pull into the driveway and stop. Charles was driving. He and Gary climbed out.

I went outside to meet them and saw an old wooden crate of some sort tied down in the pickup bed. "What's that?" I asked.

"Our boat," Charles answered.

"Whose boat?"

"*Our* boat. Yours and mine."

"We have a boat?"

"We do now."

I walked over and took a closer look. It sure didn't look like a boat. It looked like some old boards nailed together. And it was *small*. Couldn't have been more than three feet by four feet. And only a foot deep. "You call this a boat?" I said.

"Sure. And you and I are going sailing."

"Where?"

"Down that river of yours. You're out there so much, I figured it was time you really got to know it. Let's go!"

Once out on the highway, he began again. "Okay, here's the

plan. We're gonna launch this thing at the river bridge. We figure it's about ten miles over to the Scotland Bridge. At about five miles per hour, we should be there in two. Porky's gonna pick us up."

"Does your granddad know you have his truck?"

He and Gary looked at each other. "Well, sorta."

He smiled and turned up the radio. Some guy was singing about dying in a car crash before he could tell his girl he loved her. I hoped it wasn't a sign. I closed my eyes and envisioned next week's *Archer County News*:

LOCAL BOYS DIE IN BOATING MISHAP

The bodies of Jim Black and Charles Luig were pulled from the muddy Little Wichita River late yesterday after their homemade boat (not much larger than a cereal box) sank. Details are sketchy at this time, but investigators believe a giant snapping turtle may be to blame. It's been reported the victims' private parts were missing—but this has not yet been confirmed. When asked for comment, their close friend Gary Beesinger could only say, "I'm glad I didn't go."

We arrived at the river bridge and pulled off the road. Small as our boat was, it still took the three of us to carry it. We got it down the bank to the water and eased it in. It didn't just look small, it *was* small. "No way," I said.

"Sure there is," Charles rebutted. "Just get in. You first."

I shook my head and sat down in the back. Charles climbed into the front between my legs. Our knees were almost up against our chins. Gary handed us a couple of homemade paddles, pushed us off, and we were on our way.

We slowly began to drift with the muddy water. After some

initial adjustments, I wasn't *too* uncomfortable. Anyway, I tried not to think about it. Behind us, Gary wished us luck.

I must admit that, a few minutes into it, I was kind of glad I had come. We drifted along not having to paddle and just took in the sights. It was about four in the afternoon and pretty warm, but the water was cool and there was some shade along the way. It was really kind of nice. Charles opened a Coke, handed it to me, and opened one for himself. I hadn't noticed them. We sat back the best we could and enjoyed the ride.

I was just about to thank him for bringing me when we rounded the first bend.

"Bubba, do you see what I see?"

I leaned forward and looked. Directly ahead was a large cluster of water oaks overhanging the river. And amid the lower branches, just about at shoulder height, was a large maze of webs and the biggest damn spider I'd seen. It had a body the size and shape of a walnut and spindly legs about five inches long. It was black with yellow markings. I'm certain he had been waiting just for us. Charles was already paddling hard. We had time to steer clear of it, only the boat continued straight and showed no inclination of turning.

"Paddle! Harder!" I did.

It soon became evident that with its flat bottom and small size, ours was basically an uncontrollable craft.

We stopped our furious paddling to catch our breath. There were two choices. Stay put and lay low or jump. The idea of what might be *in* the muddy water wasn't appealing. So we ducked.

I lay back, and Charles crouched forward. We passed directly under the web. Charles couldn't see with his head down. I didn't want to, so I closed my eyes. We brushed against the branches, and leaves and things fell in with us. I could feel the web. After we had cleared it, we raised up and looked. We brushed twigs and such from our hair and shirts. I decided to get Charles good while I could.

"It's on you!" I shouted. Then, to my horror, I saw it *was. On his back*.

He hollered and frantically swatted behind him, managing to knock it onto me. I screamed and knocked it away. Now we were both screaming and swatting. We weren't sure where it was. The boat did everything but turn over. We finally stopped. Half afraid to look, we examined each other and searched the bottom of the boat. The spider could not be found. We tried to relax and regroup.

The river had widened out to about thirty feet, and the current was slow but steady. We got to enjoy it for five whole minutes. Then the river narrowed, and we rounded another bend. More trees. And something else. What the hell was that? It looked like a black football perched in the tree, hanging a couple of feet off the water. Our worst fears were soon realized. *River hornets*.

These hornets were bigger and meaner than any bees or wasps. There must have been a hundred of them bunched together on that nest.

We paddled at breakneck speed trying to get away from them, but to no avail. We were at the mercy of the river. "Quit paddlin'!" he said in a loud whisper. "And be still!"

"What are we gonna do?"

He whirled and looked at me. "Will you be *quiet?!* You're gonna stir 'em up!"

He was right. We were almost there. He didn't cover his head this time. He wanted to see if we were going to live or not. So did I. We froze.

. . . investigators now believe river hornets may be to blame. The victims' heads and hands were purple in color and swollen to the size of watermelons— apparently the result of hundreds of stings.

It appeared we might just skirt them. By a foot or so. We leaned as far as we could to the side and passed within eighteen inches of the nest. As we brushed the branches, their buzz increased. They were badly annoyed. I expected them to swarm all over us at any second. But they didn't. Once past them, we were too drained to celebrate.

For the next two hours, we went where the river took us. Past additional spiders, two fairly large water moccasins (or snakes of some sort), an occasional small whirlpool, and one stubborn horsefly that followed us for an hour like a tiny kamikaze pilot—dive-bombing and biting us over and over. Some scenic tour.

According to Charles's watch, it was 6:15. I felt like I had been run over by a truck. I'm sure he did, too. We had not been prepared for the river's constant meandering. Our best calculation was that we had gone about six or seven miles in all, but were still only a third of the way to the bridge. What had we gotten ourselves into?

Chapter 36

AT 8:45 P.M., we'd been on the river nearly five hours. The good news was the past hour had been incident-free. The river was at its widest. Nearly forty feet with no trees. The bad news was rigor mortis had begun to set in, *and* it was beginning to get dark. Plus we had no idea where we were.

We watched the stars come out, but unlucky for us, there was no moon. We could have used the light. We also began to hear sounds. Animals. Perhaps they were as afraid of us as we were of them. But maybe not. We rounded a bend, the first in quite a while, and the river narrowed. We strained our eyes to see.

"What is it?" I asked anxiously.

"Oh shit," he replied. "More trees." He turned and said, "Bubba, I don't have a good feeling about this."

Neither did I. I wasn't sure I could handle not being able to see what might get us.

As we neared them, we got as low as we could, covered our heads, and closed our eyes. I heard the branches scraping the front of the boat. Then Charles's shirt. Then me. What might be in them? No telling. But *something*. Something was jumping or falling from those branches and was all over us. I was certain.

I screamed. Charles screamed. I couldn't take it anymore and went over the side. And when I did, the boat turned over. I grabbed it and held on. Charles was at the other end. The water was surprisingly cold, and I could feel the current tugging at my feet. We were slowly drifting downstream. I had forgotten all about the things in the tree. I was now worried about what might be in the water just below our feet.

"*Come on!*" Charles yelled. And with that, he turned loose and began swimming toward the bank. I did the same.

I couldn't believe the current. Neither could he.

"*Damn!*" I heard him say.

I thought of something Sam had said: *I know it don't look it on top, but down below, that river's busy.* It sure was. I fought it as hard as I could. It wasn't long before my legs felt like weights. The shore was only a short distance, but it might as well have been miles. I had to rest. There was a stump nearby, and I reached for it. It was Charles's head. We both screamed, and suddenly a beam of light flashed by. And another. Then they were on us. We looked at each other. Then we heard the voices.

"*Grab the rope! It's right on top of you!*"

We grabbed and held on.

"*Hang on! We'll pull you in!*"

It was all we could do to hold on. We were exhausted. It was only twenty feet or so to the bank, but it felt like a mile. Finally, we were there.

We lay against the muddy bank and looked up into several flashlight beams. The voices returned.

"What the hell are y'all doin'? And where the hell did ya come from?"

"That *you*, Gordon?" Charles asked.

"Hell yes. Charles? Charles Luig?"

"Yeah," he managed.

"Who's with ya?"

"Jim Black," I said.

"Well kiss my ass. We thought you were frogmen or somethin'. Yeah, this here's ol' Gordon Humphrey, all right."

I recognized the name. It belonged to a local rancher. We were saved.

"What the heck are you doing out here at night?" Charles asked.

"Hell, we *were* fishin'. But it looks like you fellas have done taken care of that. Any fish that were around here are long gone by now."

Half an hour later we were headed back to town in the back of Gordon's pickup. In the cab, Gordon and his fishing buddies were laughing about the funniest thing they ever caught in the river. We didn't care. We were going home.

He dropped each of us off. They were still laughing when I climbed out. I thanked them and managed to sneak into the house unnoticed. I phoned Gary.

"What are you *doing?*" I asked. "You're supposed to be at the bridge waiting on us!"

"Where *are* you?"

"Home. Just got here."

"Are you guys all right?" he asked.

"We are now. You didn't call the sheriff, did you?"

"No, but I almost did."

"Where's the pickup?"

"I took it back to Charles's granddad's. Then I hitched a ride back to the bridge and waited another three hours. I finally gave up and came home. I figured you guys were playing a joke on me."

"I wish we *had* been. I'll tell you all about it tomorrow. Right now I'm going to take a bath and go to bed."

"Well, I'm glad you're back."

"So am I."

Chapter 37

HOW DOES a decorated highway patrolman wind up working in a poultry processing plant and dying a drunk driver?

Currents.

It's not simply a matter of having the strength to swim out of them. And wanting to. You must also know *how*. My dad didn't. He needed a light. Or rope. And got none.

Years later I would come to understand it's nobody's fault. Guilt and alcohol are two currents that, once they are caught up in them, few people escape. Especially years ago. The only people who might have helped him simply did not know how to. The sad truth is my dad had been on course for his tragic end since an early age.

I look at old photos and try to imagine what he was feeling and what must have been going through his mind at the time. I have a favorite. It's black and white and shows him sitting on the edge of the couch watching TV. Most likely *Gunsmoke* or a baseball game. I'm standing between his legs watching with him, about four years old at the time. It's the only photo I have of my dad in which he appears to be smiling.

I thought about this as I sat alone on the old water tower. I hadn't told Gary and Charles I was coming. The truth was I felt like being alone.

It was a strange night. One-half of the sky was clear, the stars twinkling Morse code to someone or each other. Perhaps to me. I wondered what message they were sending. What would they be telling me now? The sky's other half was dark, thick with clouds, lightning dancing through them. And yet there was no thunder. It was an eerie silent display. The line separating the two skies was distinct. The best I could tell, it divided Archer City down the middle. At that moment, some were seeing the stars and some the storm, perhaps from different windows of the same house.

All any of us can do in life is the best we can based on what we know. And hope that if we do get in trouble, a rope will be thrown, and we'll have the strength to take it. I'd already had one thrown to me in the river. Would there be another if I needed it? Something told me that someday I would need a strong one.

And what if someone I cared about needed one? Could I provide it? Would I know how? I hoped so. *Please let me know how.*

There was thunder for the first time. I noticed the clouds had grown more ominous. The wind was picking up, and the first few drops of rain pinged against the railing. I didn't want to think what Mom would say if she knew I was up there.

I thought about Sam's granddad and death's mirror. I wondered if my dad *could* see me now. If so, what would he be thinking?

I looked out over my hometown as we had so often done. I could see my house, where Mom was probably washing clothes. Charles and Gary were out there somewhere. So were Sam and Rose. And Harley. And on a hill eleven miles away, Lorrie. My heart was scattered in the River Big. I wondered if somehow one day I could make it all fit together.

I reached into my back pocket and removed a flare. It was starting to rain harder now. I taped it to the outside of the railing and lit it. I stood watching it, then climbed down and started home. Behind me, the beacon burned brightly only at times, as it struggled against the wind and rain. Summer was drawing to a close.

Part Four

END OF SUMMER

Chapter 38

CHARLES AND I SAT on his front porch drinking grape Kool-Aid. We had just finished mowing his yard. "More in here if you boys need it," his mom said through the window screen.

"Thanks," I answered back. I looked at him. "Well, our yard-mowing is just about over for the year. What are you going to do with all your money?" I asked.

"Get a new lawn mower for next year," he replied.

I laughed.

"Aren't you?" he said.

I thought about it. "Yeah, I guess so." I looked over at him. "Wait a minute. Let me get this straight. We work our tails off all summer wearing out one mower just so we can buy another?"

"I reckon," he answered.

"When do we get ahead?"

"When we stop runnin' over faucets and tools and crap, I guess. That's why I took on a second job."

"Sounds like we need better clients. Maybe we should be mowing grass in Wichita Falls."

"Naw, I heard those people over there are real particular about their yards."

"You're making me depressed," I said.

"I'll be right back," he suddenly said. He jumped up and took off.

Shortly, he returned with a rake and some newspapers and matches.

"What are you doing?" I asked.

"Wasp nest," he replied, motioning to the house eaves above us.

The nest was a new one with only four or five wasps on it. Charles wrapped the paper around the end of the rake and lit it. When the flames were big, he held it to the nest, and the wasps immediately fell to the porch, minus their wings. As they spun around on the concrete, he smashed each with his shoe, then reached up and knocked down the nest and set it on fire. We watched it burn. He left to put out the paper with the hose, and I stood there looking at the remains. I was glad they were gone. I hate the darn things. Still, there was something about the suddenness of it all. One moment they were there doing whatever it is wasps do, and the next, their whole world was gone. *Just like that*. At that moment, his sister Karen came out the front door. Boy, was I thankful. I didn't want to have to think about it anymore. Now I wouldn't have to, because she was awfully cute. So I pushed it out of my mind. The best I could.

Chapter 39

BILLY CONKLIN was holding court in a back booth at Joe's Drive-in. "The way I heard it, he just showed up at the hospital late a couple of nights ago, soaking wet, his lungs half filled with water. My aunt says it's a wonder he hadn't drowned. They say he was scared crazy, but that ain't nothin', 'cause he's already nuts. Anyway, they got the water outta him, and next thing they know, he's up and gone. Just like that. Crazy bastard."

Charles and Gary looked at me. We were two booths over, but Billy was making sure everyone in there heard.

"And then yesterday Rooster and Cartwright are out there fishin', and he comes up outta nowhere and scares the shit out of 'em. They say he was just runnin' back and forth across the bank tellin' 'em to watch the river. Told 'em over and over to keep watchin' it whatever they did. Then he just run off."

"What did they do?" someone asked.

"Hell, at first they thought it was funny. But Cartwright said it got damn eerie after a while, even if it *was* Harley."

Charles took a swig of his Coke and set it down. "You believe that shit?" he asked.

Before Gary could say no, I said yes. They both looked at me.

"He did it to me this morning," I said. "And I have to say, it scared the daylights out of me, too."

"You're kidding."

"Nope. I'm not. I was fishing, waiting for Sam, daydreaming, and all of a sudden here comes this voice from behind me. 'Keep yer eye on this river, you hear? Keep yer eye on it, now.'

I spun around and there he was. Pacing back and forth. Eyes on the water. Real nervous-like. I tried to talk to him, but I don't think he remembered who I was. It was like I wasn't even there. He might have even been talking to himself. And all he kept saying was, 'Keep yer eye on this river, you hear? Keep yer eye on it, now.' Next thing I knew, he was gone."

"*That* is weird," Charles said.

Gary hadn't said a word. He clearly was spooked.

"And no one knows what brought this on?" Charles asked.

"Not really," I answered. "Sam did tell me Harley showed up at his house the night Billy's talking about. The night he nearly drowned. Evidently he went straight to Sam's from the hospital. Sam said he'd never seen him that bad off. He tried to talk to him, but just like with me, he wasn't paying Sam no mind. Just walked back and forth on the porch mumbling to himself. Then he left."

They were both staring at me.

"What was he saying?" Gary asked. "Did Sam hear him?"

I nodded. "Sam told me he just kept repeating it over and over even as he walked away. The same two words: '*I'm sorry.*' He just kept saying, '*I'm sorry.*'"

Gary dropped his french fry. Charles sipped his Coke.

"It upset Sam something terrible."

"What does *he* think happened?"

"He says something definitely happened to Harley out there on the river the other night, but most likely we'll never know what."

I took a drink of my Coke. "I will tell you this—and I'm not saying it to make you guys feel bad or anything. Sam told me there's something we all need to think about when we try to figure Harley. He says loneliness is a thief that has robbed Harley blind. Not the kind we sometimes feel—but *real* loneliness.

The mean kind. Loneliness has taken more from Harley than we'll ever know, he says."

"You don't suppose that's what Harley meant when he told you the reason he walks at night is because he hurts and can't sleep?" Gary asked. "That maybe he was talking about being alone?"

Charles and I looked at him. For a moment, none of us spoke. Then Billy Conklin broke the silence.

"As far as I'm concerned, he's got to go," he was saying to anyone who would listen. "That retard has finally gone off the deep end, and we can't have him around here no more. There ain't no tellin' what he's liable to do."

"He hasn't hurt anyone," someone said.

"Yeah, but he sure as hell might. And then you'll be sorry."

"You can't just run him out of town."

"The hell I can't."

"What's it matter to *you*, anyway?"

All heads turned our way. Gary looked as surprised as everyone. The words had come from his mouth.

"Well, if it ain't Porky and his faggot friends. What was that you said?"

"You heard him, asshole." Charles answered.

"What did you call me?" Billy said as he stood up.

"You're not deaf," Charles replied.

Billy glared at him. Then at Gary. Then at me. He knew any fight right now would involve the four of us. He was thinking. So were we. He was clearly bigger and stronger than any of us, but I was hopeful that at some point Gary and I could get him down and hold him while Charles worked him over. And he would.

He might have reached the same conclusion. Maybe not. It didn't matter, because Joe had appeared.

"Billy, I believe you're done eating, so you best be on your way."

Billy stared at Joe, who was a couple of inches taller than him and thirty years older. You could see the wheels spinning in Billy's head.

"If you don't leave right now, you'll not be welcomed in here again."

Whether Billy decided Joe might be more than he bargained for, or that he would, in fact, have to eat again someday, he turned and stomped out the door without looking back.

Joe walked over. We four looked out the window. Billy was in the parking lot kicking the gravel and shooting glances at the door.

"No sense in you all rushing off. Shakes on the house today," he said. "The usual flavors?" he asked.

We smiled.

After he left, I looked at Gary. "What was that all about?" I asked. "Now all of a sudden you're a tough guy?"

"What about *him?*" he said, motioning to Charles.

"I was coming to your rescue."

"Who said I needed help?"

"Didn't you?" Charles and I asked in unison.

"No! Not then, anyway. Now, maybe if he'd have come over here . . ."

We laughed, and Joe returned with our shakes. We dove in.

Later, as we were finishing up, I looked out the window.

Billy was gone.

Chapter 40

I MUST CONFESS to hanging around the house the next couple of days and keeping an eye out when I did go anywhere. But by the third day, I finally said to heck with it. If Billy was going to get me, so be it. I made this bold decision sitting at the red light on my Husky and was even thinking about driving past his house. Suddenly, behind me, there was some commotion over at the jailhouse. Next thing I knew, Sheriff Harris's car sped past headed west, siren blaring. And behind him, Deputy Don. I set out in hot pursuit. At the edge of town, they turned south toward the baseball field. I followed them to Harley's. There was a handful of people in the yard when we arrived, and it wasn't long before I knew. *Harley was dead.*

Evidently, a night or two ago, he drank some turpentine. Nearly a pint. His possessions, for the most part, totaled thirty dollars in cash, a transistor radio without batteries, numerous sketches of birds with the initials *H. H.* on them, and a map of California. Hard to figure, they said. Then again, not really. After all, he *was* nuts.

I climbed back on my Husky and headed to Sam's. He and Rose were sitting on the porch when I finally arrived. Sam stood and smiled as I walked up.

"How's my good friend today?" he asked. He looked at me, and his smile faded. He waited for me to speak.

"Harold's dead," I softly said.

Rose dropped her head down and stared into her lap. Sam looked away.

"An accident?" he asked.

I shook my head. Neither of them looked at me.

Normally, Rose went inside and left Sam and me to sit on the porch. Today, she sat with us. Rocking. Sobbing. Finally, she spoke. "I just can't help but think that whatever happened out there on the river that night had something to do with this."

I looked at Sam. He sat on the edge of the porch, as he had for a while now, just staring at the ground. He said nothing.

I knew what he was thinking. It wasn't the river. And it wasn't Billy Conklin, or anybody else in town, for that matter. It was the thief who came in the night and kept coming till Harley had nothing else whatsoever to give. Then he came again.

Rose broke the silence. "At least we can cherish the thought of him in heaven as we speak. Thank the Lord for that. Praise God."

I looked at her and smiled. She smiled back, big, through her tears. "I wonder what he's doing right now," she wondered aloud.

"Flying," Sam said, without looking up.

She and I turned and looked at him.

"Darlin'," he said, "if God *is* in heaven, then that's what Harold's doin' right now. He told me once that was what he wanted more than anything. *To be a bird*. He wanted to be able to sing real pretty and fly high above the town wild and free, just lookin' down at all the people without havin' to be with 'em." He paused. "And not just any bird. Nope, he wanted to be one of them that fly to California every year. To that town."

"Capistrano?" I offered. I remembered reading about it in school.

He looked at me and smiled. "That's it. He told me how they go home year after year. That's what he wanted most. To have a real home to go to. He might have lived here all his life, but this was never his home."

"Then that's what we shall pray for," Rose said. She closed her eyes and began to hum a familiar hymn.

Sam got up and walked toward the river.

I watched him go.

Chapter 41

THIS WAS IT. Our big finale. We'd been planning it for some time—a three-day campout our mothers had reluctantly agreed to, on the conditions that we promised to stay on dry land and out of trouble. The hot weather was pretty much over, and the nights were getting downright cool, which was just perfect. We rode our scooters out to the river, parked them under the bridge high on the bank, and hiked east. When the trail finally petered out, we made our own and went another couple of miles before settling on a site. After scouring it good for anything remotely resembling a bug, rodent, or reptile, we set up camp—fairly certain there was no Bigfoot, or ostriches within a hundred miles or so, although you can never really be sure about those things.

"When are we gonna eat?" Gary wanted to know

"It's only four o'clock!" I said. "Just get you a Snickers out of the ice chest. In fact, get us all one. And a Coke. He did so, as Charles and I unpacked everything and laid out our bedrolls. After we finished our candy bars and sodas, we gathered firewood and then went down to the bank, some thirty feet away, and fished.

"Think we'll catch anything?" Gary asked.

"I might," I said, "but you guys won't."

They both looked over. "Why's that?" he asked.

" 'Cause I'm using kidney and you're using shrimp. And shrimp won't get the job done."

"That so?"

"Yeah. And your sinkers aren't big enough, either."

"How do *you* know?"

"What do you think Sam and I've been doin' out here all summer? Just killing time?"

"We'll see about that, Bubba," Charles said.

A thought hit me. "You think our scooters will be all right parked where they're at?"

"Yeah," he said. "No one'll be able to get yours started, and everyone knows better than to mess with mine."

"Yeah, right," Gary said. "Well, next summer when my uncle gives me his car, *I'll* be a big shot."

"What car?" Charles asked.

"His Oldsmobile. He's gettin' a new one."

"That old orange thing?"

"It's not orange!"

"Well, what color would *you* call rust?"

"Okay, we'll remember that when you want to ride in it, won't we, Jim?"

I didn't answer.

"Will you quit thinking about her?" Charles said.

I looked over at him.

"That's over, remember? Heck, it never even got off the ground."

"I don't know," I said. "I've been thinking lately that maybe I jumped the gun. I mean, what if that cowboy she was sitting by was just another one of her cousins?"

"Could be," Gary offered. "She's probably got about a hundred."

"I doubt it," Charles was quick to answer. "Most of those people over there are dairy farmers. Most likely he was from Joy or Petrolia."

"Yeah, I guess you're right," I said dejectedly.

"Bubba, your best bet is to forget about her and move on."

"I agree," Gary added. "You'll find somebody one of these years." He and Charles laughed. I decided to take their advice. At least for the time being.

We sat and fished till suppertime. They didn't catch a thing. I did, but only a six-inch pollywog. They were not impressed. The next day we tried again but with similar results. And again, I had our only catch—a small soft-shelled turtle, which we also released. Tired of fishing, we spent our final day hiking and exploring. Gary found part of an old cow skull, and spent the afternoon trying to convince Charles and me it was something more sinister. We finally agreed, mostly because the lower jaw was missing and it did look pretty strange. Worn out from all the walking, we set out our fishing lines, fixed supper, and crashed.

The rest of the world was a million miles away. The night sky was so full of stars that it seemed as if they would surely begin to spill out and fall for real. Our campfire burned softly, and our bellies were full of stew and crackers, fried pies and Cokes. The radio was on, and Gary Puckett was singing about a young girl and telling her to get out of his mind. (My thoughts exactly.) It was late as we lay on our sleeping bags. No one had spoken in a while when Charles broke the silence.

"I still don't know how he drank that damn turpentine. He must've been one tough guy."

"I can't even stand the smell of it," Gary added.

Charles sat up. "I believe I'd have had to use a gun. I mean, really, how the hell do you *drink* that stuff?"

"I guess you just have to want to bad enough," I said.

"I guess," he replied. "And what was the deal with all the bird pictures? Anybody hear?"

"*He* drew them," I answered. "Those were his initials on them. Anyway, Sam and Rose have a couple he gave them."

"No kidding? Who'd have thought it? I'll bet no one else knew he could draw like that."

"Probably not."

"That's a damn shame," he said.

I watched him stir the fire and lay back down. For an hour, no one spoke.

I think Gary was asleep. I don't know about Charles. As for me, I was close, but still feeling a little sad after our conversation about Harley. Lying there, I was thinking I wanted to tell Gary and Charles I loved them. Because I did. But I couldn't bring myself to do it. It's just not something thirteen-year-old friends do—especially guys. And that made me sadder still. I closed my eyes and tried to forget about it. I had barely gotten to sleep when all hell broke loose.

"Tarantula!" Charles was screaming. I opened my eyes. He was up and jumping around, slapping himself all over. *"Tarantulas! Everywhere! Look out!"*

I was certain I was covered. Gary and I flew up off our sleeping bags, swatting at our clothes and yelling, our brains trying hard to process just who had yelled first and what were the chances this was on the up and up. That took a few seconds. By then, Charles was already dying laughing.

"Dammit, Charles!" we cussed. "That's not funny."

He clearly disagreed, because he was still bent over, holding his side and trying to catch his breath. I loved him, all right, but I could have killed him.

Finally, we laughed, too. "Damn, guys," he said. "I had to do *something*. You were fizzling out too early. It's our last time out before school, remember? You can *always* sleep."

He was right. We could sleep at home. "Hey, we might as well check our lines while we're up," I said.

"Yeah. Fish for breakfast sounds pretty good." Gary said. He grabbed the flashlight, and we started down the bank. "I'll bring the lantern as soon as I pee," Charles said.

"Keep an eye on him," I told Gary as we reached the water's edge. We stared at the bank, realizing there were only two poles. *Mine was missing.*

Gary shone the light up and down the bank. "There it is!" he said, pointing some twenty feet away. I ran over and grabbed it. The rod doubled over when I raised it up and pulled.

It seemed to be hung.

I tried to jiggle it free but couldn't. Then I felt a movement. I remembered stories of huge catfish taken from the river in years past—some supposedly near a hundred pounds. I was really excited, and Gary sensed it. "What is it? Have we got something?" he asked.

"I sure do! I told you guys you had the wrong bait!" It was coming, but slowly. It was something, all right. Something big. "You're not gonna believe *this*," I said. "Here, hold my pole." Gary took it from me, and I reached down and grabbed the line. I pulled hard with both hands, and it finally broke the surface. At first we didn't know what it was. Then we saw.

It was a man's head.

Chapter 42

GARY AND I SCREAMED and ran over each other trying to get up the bank, where we ran flush into Charles.

"What the hell's going on?" he asked, grabbing the lantern.

My heart was racing, and I could hardly breathe. Gary was sucking on his inhaler.

"It's a body!" I said. And I began looking around us in all directions, half expecting I didn't know what.

"Come on," he said. "You're not pullin' that on me."

"He ain't lying," Gary said. "It's a friggin' body. *No kidding!"*

"Well, I just can't believe you guys think I'd fall for something like that."

"We're not! I swear! *Let's get outta here!"*

"Aw, it's probably just an old tree limb or something," he said as he moved past us and started down the bank. "Let *me* see that sucker."

I wanted to stop him, but it was too late. He had set the lantern down and already had the line and was pulling. We held our breath and watched over his shoulder. Suddenly there it was.

"Damn! You weren't kidding! Come down here and hold the light for a second."

"No way!" I said.

"Come on, dadgum it. I can't see!

"For somebody who was scared of an ostrich, you sure are brave now," I pointed out.

"That was different," he said. "We didn't know what the heck that was."

I hesitated, then reluctantly climbed down, with Gary following close behind. I grabbed the lantern and knelt beside him, then held it out. There were patches where handfuls of the man's hair were missing.

Charles pulled him up the best he could, and for the first time, we saw his face. He was bleached white and badly bloated. He was hooked through one cheek, with the rusty stem of the large fishhook protruding from his mouth. Chunks of flesh were gone from his face—perhaps eaten by turtles or snakes. We all just stared without speaking. Charles leaned closer as if he'd noticed something. Then . . .

"Look out!" he yelled. He must have even scared himself, because the three of us nearly killed one another trying to get back up the bank. The body slowly sank back into the muddy water and disappeared.

"Gosh amighty!" I yelled. *"Will you stop that?"*

"I say we throw him in the river!" Gary said.

"We ought to!" I agreed.

Charles still had one good joke left in him. "Okay, here's what we'll do—Gary, you stay here with it, while Jim and I—" He never finished.

Gary grabbed both our shirts. "Bullcrap! I ain't lettin' the two of you outta my sight!" And he meant it.

We finally agreed to hike back to the highway, ride into town, and report it to the sheriff. With Charles holding the lantern, me the flashlight, and Gary our shirttails, we headed off.

It was nearly four in the morning when we finally got there, and just about sunup by the time we got back. We were joined by Sheriff Harris, Deputy Don, and Clyde Long, the game warden. After a search of the surrounding area, they wrapped the body in a tarp and carried it all the way back to the highway. It was ten o'clock before we all got back to the jailhouse and Sheriff Harris finally said we could go. We climbed aboard our Cushmans and headed for Joe's. We were starved.

There, we dove into our Rancher's Breakfast Specials and relived our adventure. An hour later, Deputy Don showed up and sat down in our booth.

"Thought you boys might be interested in knowin' just who it was you found out there. Turns out his name is Stanton Miller from Electra. Been missin' a couple of weeks now. Seems there was some trouble between him and some woman's husband. I guess you could say foul play is suspected. Anyway, sheriff asked me to personally thank you again."

"Think we'll get our picture in the Archer paper?" Gary asked.

"I'll bet that can be arranged," he said, smiling. "Anyhow, breakfast is on the department."

We thanked him as he left, and laughed and slapped each other on the back.

"Well, what do you know about that?" Gary said. "We're famous."

"Porky, you've *always* been famous. You just don't know it," Charles kidded.

Deputy Don had stopped at the door. "Oh, I almost forgot," he was saying. "We found another fishhook in him. Snagged in his britches. Seems you guys weren't the first to catch him."

We looked at each other.

"Sheriff says he could have gotten it anywhere along the river. But you know what I think? I think that hook belonged to Harley. I think Harley hung him upriver the night he nearly drowned. Wouldn't thata been a sight to see?" He paused, thinking. "No way of knowin' for sure, I reckon. And I guess it don't really matter now. But that would explain him warnin' everybody to watch the river." He looked at us and smiled. "Anyway, that's what I believe. Well, you boys take it easy." And out he went.

Chapter 43

WHEN I GOT HOME, Mom met me at the front door. "Well, did you have a good time?"

"Yeah, we really did," I said as I dropped my stuff on the porch.

"You look exhausted. Did you get any sleep?"

"Nope. You won't believe what all happened."

"Honey, something happened *here* while you were gone. I hate to have to tell you this. I've been worried sick about it."

"What is it?" I asked.

"Rose died. I just heard about it this morning at the post office. A rattlesnake bit her while she was hanging out clothes."

"What?"

"It was windy, and she never heard it. It happened the day before yesterday. I haven't heard how Sam's doing."

"I've got to go," I said, tears welling in my eyes.

"I know. You go ahead. But be careful, hear? I worry about you on that scooter."

"I'm okay," I said as I started it and climbed on.

"I guess you're all Sam's got left," she said as I drove away.

I headed north through town. I was scared. Losing Tick and Harley was bad enough. Now Rose was gone. He was out there somewhere all alone, and I hated the thought of it. I was angry. What had he ever done to deserve this? He'd better be all right. Dammit, he'd better be okay.

Suddenly I was crying. I could barely see to drive. *Please* let him be all right. *Somebody, please.*

I passed the Muleshoe Ranch and soon after pulled off the highway at the river and skidded to a stop. I jumped off and ran down the trail toward his house as hard as I could go. It wasn't long before I reached our fishing spot. I stopped to check there first, and there he was, sitting on the bank staring at the water. I paused to catch my breath, then made my way down the bank and sat beside him. He didn't look over, but instead just kept staring ahead.

"I'm sorry," I said as my tears returned. "I'm so sorry."

He didn't answer.

"It just ain't right," I said. "It's so unfair. Life is so unfair."

"It's somethin' else, all right," he said softly. "That's for sure."

"I'm sorry I wasn't here."

He looked over at me. He had been crying, too.

"Wasn't nothin' you coulda done, son," he said. "Nothin' nobody coulda done."

I stared at the muddy water. I wondered what hidden things were passing in front of us without our knowing. *Living things.* Breathing. Thinking. Loving. Grieving. I looked down, and for the first time noticed the old battered suitcase.

"Are you going somewhere?" I asked.

"Yes, son, I am," he said. I'm leavin'. I gotta get away. There just ain't nothin' left for me here."

"I'm here," I said, my eyes refilling with tears.

"I know, son," he answered, looking over at me. "I didn't mean it that way. You're mighty important to me. *Mighty* important. You're the reason I'm here now. I'd have already gone, but I came back to say goodbye—I couldn't leave without sayin' goodbye to my good friend."

"I'd never have forgiven you," I said.

"I don't believe that. I really don't. But I couldn't risk it."

"What about your house and things?"

"Ain't a thing back there worth much. Least of all that old shack. 'Bout all I'm leavin' behind are memories."

"We had some good times, didn't we?"

"Yes, son, we sure did. And I'm takin' those with me. And you do the same. You hang on to those that you have. You carry the good ones with you always. They'll come in handy someday, you remember that."

"I will," I promised.

"And I want you to remember somethin' else. Listen close, now. Someday you may look back on this and think I let you down—that I quit on you. That ain't so. You mean everything to me. More than you'll ever know. You always remember that, and when the time comes, try and understand. Will you do that, son?"

I nodded and looked down. A tear hung from my chin. I started to wipe it away when it fell. It broke into a hundred tiny tears.

Sam stood up.

"I always liked seein' this little river run," he said. "It weren't the fish. And it sure ain't much to look at. I guess maybe it's because it just never seemed as lonely around here when there was water in it. Anyway, I'll miss it, that's for sure." He turned and looked north up the highway and toward Wichita.

"Where will you go?" I asked.

"I believe I'll go back to Birmingham," he answered. "Maybe take in a game at that little ballpark where I first laid eyes on my Rose. If it's still there."

I got up. "Are you coming back?"

He looked at me and said, "No, son. I reckon not."

Then he picked up his suitcase with one hand and held the

other out to me. "Mr. Jim Black, sir, it has been an honor and a privilege."

I took his hand. It occurred to me this was the first time we had ever touched. I was surprised at how soft his hand was. I squeezed it long and hard. I was crying hard now, and suddenly his hand was not enough. I put my arms around him. He put the suitcase down and hugged me back.

"I love you, Sam," I said.

He didn't answer. He didn't have to. He was crying, too.

My mind was racing. I thought about the first time I met him. And Rose. And Harley. I thought about my mom. And my dad. And Charles and Gary. Lorrie. Then it hit me. I saw it clear, just for a moment. I let go of Sam and stepped back.

"This is what it's all about, isn't it?" I asked. "The River Big—*this is what it's all about.*"

He looked at me for a moment, then away, toward town and beyond. I waited for his answer. Finally, it came.

"No, son," he said. "I 'spect it's still more than just this."

I was disappointed.

Then, perhaps sensing my disappointment, he looked back at me. "Then again, I reckon that's somethin' we each have to decide for ourselves."

I thought about that for a moment. I looked at him and smiled. He smiled back, and pulled me close, and we hugged one last time. Then he picked up his suitcase and started up the bank.

"Goodbye, Sam," I managed to say.

He stopped when he reached the top and looked back. First at the river, then at me.

"Goodbye, son," he said. And he walked away.

I stood there for a while, watching the river—the slow-moving water reminding me once more of things past and those still to come. Finally, I dried my eyes and made my way up the bank. I expected to see Sam out there, on the shoulder, walking down the highway. I didn't. He was nowhere in sight. My friend was gone.

Chapter 44

AS I RODE INTO TOWN, I spotted Charles's Eagle at the barbershop and decided to stop. Sure enough, when I walked in, Coot was working on him. I noticed Hank and Johnny playing checkers as usual. Behind them, Billy Conklin was doing what he usually did.

"Hi there, young-un," Coot said. "Have a seat there, and soon as I finish ruinin' my best clippers on Romeo here, I'll be right with you."

"I don't need a haircut," I said.

Charles winked at me and asked, "You ever think about sharpening those things?"

"That's not the problem," Coot said. "The problem is they weren't made for cuttin' steel wool."

"Well, could you at least get my sideburns even today? I'm tired of Porky ribbing me."

"Hell, no one's left here in twenty years with even sideburns," Hank kidded.

"More like thirty," Johnny added.

Coot smiled. "You might leave here with one less ear if you're not careful. And if you don't study up on the benefits of the occasional use of soap and water, you won't have to worry at all about how you look to women."

"We've been camping," Charles said. I wondered if he had told them about the body.

"Where at, the dump ground?" Coot replied.

They all laughed, and then Hank looked up at me and said, "Guess you heard about your friend by now?"

The laughter stopped. "Yes," I said.

"Damn shame," Coot said, shaking his head.

"What happened?" Charles asked.

Evidently he hadn't heard. "Rose stepped on a rattlesnake while we were gone," I said. "She died."

"No kidding?" he said.

"No shit," Billy answered loudly. "And that ain't all. Scared her so bad, she fell right on top of him. You'd think thata killed him, fat as that bitch was, but all it did was make him mad. They say it bit her forty times."

"We can do without that," Coot said.

"I'm glad to be rid of 'em, myself," Billy then said. "We didn't need them around here anyway. Hell, I never did trust 'em."

"Is Sam gone, too?" Charles asked.

"Gone to Alabama," I said. "Back to Birmingham."

They all stopped what they were doing and looked at me.

"What the hell are you talkin' about?" Billy asked.

"That's where Sam said he was going."

He laughed. "Hell, I knew you were nuts for hangin' around that nigger, but you're crazier than I thought. That coon's dead."

"What?" I asked.

"He shot himself, young-un," Coot said. "I guess finding Rose like that was just too much. I thought you knew."

Suddenly the room felt hot.

"I'll say he shot himself! Blew a hole in his chest the size of a cantaloupe. They say he'd sawed off that Long Tom twelve-gauge of his to where it wasn't two foot long—so's he could reach the trigger."

"Why don't you just hush up?" Johnny said. "You weren't there."

"Don't matter. I heard Alvin talkin' 'bout it down at the fire station. They say the whole left side of his chest was gone. Probably blew his damn heart right out in the river. Alvin said some catfish probably had it for supper, but I told him, hell, even a catfish wouldn't eat a nigger's heart. But a turtle might. A damned old turtle will eat anything."

"Will you pipe down?" Coot said. "Now, Johnny's asked you once, and I'm not going to ask you again. This is still my barbershop. You hear me?"

This had to be a dream.

"I don't understand," I said to Coot. "I was just talking to him a little while ago."

"Young-un, that just can't be," he answered. The others were all staring at me. Even Charles. "Cartwright and Rooster found him last evening when they were out there fishin'. He hadn't been dead long."

I felt my throat tighten and my eyes well up. Billy noticed.

"And you know what?" he said. "No one gives a shit."

"That ain't so," I said.

"You know why? 'Cause they were worthless. That damn Harley, too."

"Don't say that," I said, standing up, my eyes spilling.

Billy stood and walked over. "They weren't nothin' but a bunch of damn strays—ever' one of 'em. Hell, they didn't deserve to live."

That was more than I could bear. The next thing I knew, I was on him. Hitting him. I couldn't see him for the tears, so I just swung wildly. No one moved. I hit him for Sam. And Rose. Harley. Even Charles and Gary. And I hit him for me. And I kept hitting him. Hard.

"*You're* the worthless one," I said. "You think anyone gives a shit about you? Nobody's *ever* cared about you. *Nobody*. Not even your mom or dad. *You're* the damn stray in this town." Then I stopped. I realized what I'd said. I looked at him. His eyes were closed tight, his face red and bleeding. A single tear trailed from one eye. I started to climb off when I felt a jolt, and suddenly everything went black. When I opened my eyes, Billy was on top of me. I could see Coot bent over him, his large forearm pulled tight against Billy's neck. Hank and Johnny each held one of his arms. A mixture of blood and snot hung from his lip. Beside me lay the heavy glass ashtray he'd hit me with. Charles picked it up and drew it back, staring at Billy.

"Bubba, you just tell me, and I'll show him what this feels like. *I swear to God I will.*"

And he would have. Even he was about to cry, something I'd never seen him do. He looked down at me, and I slowly shook my head.

Coot pulled harder against Billy's throat, cutting off his air.

"Listen to me, Billy," he said, "I'm not lettin' go till you stop struggling. You hear me?"

Billy relaxed a little and nodded. My head was killing me.

"We're going to stand up now, and if you so much as flinch, Hank and Johnny and I are going to make you wish you hadn't. You understand that?"

Billy nodded again, and together they slowly rose. The three men held on tight. Charles helped me sit up. My side hurt like hell. He must have been kicking or hitting me before they managed to restrain him.

"There's some wash rags on the counter over there," Coot said, motioning. "Better get one, he's bleeding pretty good."

Charles did so and wiped my face. "How bad is it?" I asked.

"Well, you looked a whole lot better five minutes ago," he said.

I managed to smile.

He went to the sink and got a clean cloth and wet it. He held it tight against my head. The coolness felt good.

"We're lettin' go now, Billy," Coot was saying. "And when we do, you're gonna walk right on outta here. And don't you come back for some time. You hear me?"

"Okay, okay," he replied.

They slowly released him. Billy wiped his nose. He glared at me and then turned and walked to the door and stopped. "I'm not the one who should be leavin'. *He's* the damn troublemaker. Always has been." He looked at me. "Talkin' to Sambone, were you? Well, that either makes you a lyin' bastard or a crazy one. 'Cause if you were, you were talkin' to one dead nigger. You hear me? *One damned old crazy dead nigger.*"

Chapter 45

THE COUNTY BURIED SAM the next day. I watched from a distance as two filthy workers slid his plywood coffin from a flatbed truck and dropped it into the ground. They then jumped into the truck and sped away. A third worker, fat, in faded overalls, who had been sitting on a backhoe cussing the other two, began filling the shallow grave. He chewed tobacco and spat as he worked. The wind had suddenly picked up, and most of the juice found his boots or the side of the John Deere. Some of it landed in Sam's grave. Finally, he finished and drove away.

I walked over. Sam was buried next to Rose. Their graves were located in the far northwest corner of the cemetery, away from any flowers or trees. I looked down and was surprised to see a headstone between them. It was laid flat in the ground facing up and read simply: WASHINGTON. Out of the corner of my eye, I saw someone approaching. It was Coot. He was carrying a plastic wreath in one hand and a brown paper bag in the other. He walked up and looked at the bandage on my forehead.

"You okay?" he asked.

I nodded. It had taken four stitches to close the cut. Today the spot looked like I'd been hit by one of Danny Joe's fastballs. Felt like it, too.

"Maybe you should've let Charles hit him with that ashtray."

"I don't know," I said. "I think maybe Billy's been hurt enough."

He shot me a quizzical look and then stared down at the headstone.

"Damn, that thing looks even smaller out here than it did in town," he said.

"Did *you* buy it?" I asked.

He nodded. "Hell, everybody deserves to be remembered."

He bent down and placed the wreath on the grave. We stood for a moment without saying anything. Then he spoke. " 'Fore I forget it, this is for you," he said, reaching into the bag. "We found it when we went through his house. There was a note attached—said he wanted you to have it." He handed it to me.

It was Sam's ball glove.

I reached out and took it. I held it to my face and breathed deep, taking in its distinct smell.

"We couldn't figure out that name on the side. I never knew anyone to call him that."

"That's where Satchel Paige signed it," I said. "He used to pitch with Satch in the Negro Leagues."

"You don't say?"

"Didn't he ever tell you? I figured he would have told you," I said.

"I guess he did, but hell, I never believed him." He looked away, then at his watch. "Well, gotta go. Got hair to cut. You need a ride, son?"

Sam used to call me that.

"No thank you," I said. "I'm fine."

"Okay, well, stay outta trouble." He then smiled, winked, and left.

I watched him walk away. Suddenly I felt cold. The wind was out of the north now, the sky a cast-iron gray. The first cold front of the season was pushing through. I stood for a moment looking out across the cemetery. All the crosses. All the headstones. All the lives. I heard a faint squawking sound. For a moment, I couldn't place it. Finally, I looked up. Above me, a large group of geese were flying south. They formed a huge V—there must have been forty or fifty of them. I noticed three or four vacant spots in their formation. I remembered hearing once that when a goose dies or goes missing, they leave the vacancy unfilled—maybe in hopes that the bird will return to fill it. Or perhaps just in its memory.

I followed them until they were out of sight. I looked down at the glove, and I knew I would never wear it again.

I heard a noise and turned around. Charles and Gary were standing behind me.

"Hey, Bubba," Charles said.

"What are y'all doing here?" I asked.

"Came to get you," he answered. "Raylette loaned us her car. For real. We're going to Wichita to get some pizza and maybe play some miniature golf."

"I don't know," I said.

"We're not taking no for an answer. You're going."

"How did you guys know I was here?"

"Your mom told us you might be out here," Gary said. "She's worried about you."

"I saw him. I really did. He was standing right in front of me. I know that must sound crazy."

"We believe you," they said.

I began to cry.

"He said he came back to say goodbye. Said he couldn't leave without saying goodbye."

I paused and looked away. I noticed a dark line of thunderstorms beginning to build to the southwest. Finally, I looked back at them. "Did I ever tell you guys about the River Big?" I asked.

"No, but you probably will," Charles said, grinning.

"I'd like to, I really would."

"Then let's go. You can tell us over pizza and Cokes.

"Thanks, guys," I said.

"Don't mention it," Gary replied. "Besides, you're buying." And they laughed.

"No, I mean it," I said. *"Thanks."*

A gust of wind came up and forced me to fasten my jacket. I placed the glove under my arm and stared down at the head-stone one last time. WASHINGTON. Then I dug my hands deep into my pockets.

"I love you guys."

They both looked at me for the longest time. Then Gary smiled and threw his arm around my shoulder. Charles did the same.

"After all, Bubba," he said, "what are friends for?"

And with that, we headed off, leaving Sam and that summer behind. But never very far away.

In the distance, the approaching rainstorm moved closer, promising to fill the banks we'd climbed.

Epilogue

THAT WAS MORE THAN thirty years ago. I don't know what happened on the river that day, but this much I do know—Samuel Joseph Washington died of a broken heart.

Life, Sam once said, *is somethin' else.* And it is. Ten years passed before Lorrie and I crossed paths again. She was living in Dallas studying to be a nurse. We dated for a while, it didn't work out, and we went our separate ways. Then, when I turned forty, I wrote to her. She wrote back, and three years later we were married. Sam was right. *Sometimes it just takes time.*

Charles and Gary exist to this day. Time has changed us, but not our friendship. And for that, I am grateful. These days, when we are lucky enough to be together, we laugh and reminisce about those magical times.

Joe and Coot are gone now. They died some years back, within weeks of each other, their hearts having just played out. The drive-in and barbershop went through a series of new owners but were never the same again. Today, each sits vacant.

And finally, in 1970, Billy Conklin left Archer City to "see the world" and "kill some gooks." He returned a year later, leaving an arm and a leg behind in a rice paddy somewhere in Southeast Asia. Today, he spends his days sitting by the Veterans' Memorial on the courthouse square. At night, he hobbles through the streets of Archer. Some say he's a Peeping Tom.

I returned to the river recently. Lorrie and I had been to Archer to visit my mom. I slowed as we neared the river bridge, then pulled off the highway and parked. She looked up from her Jan Karon paperback. "There's something I want to take a look at," I said.

"Want me to come?" she asked.

"No, I'll just be a minute."

She smiled, and I got out and started down what used to be the path to our fishing spot. Once there, everything looked different. The river was almost completely obscured by a thick growth of willows and water oaks. Our old spot was difficult to find and inaccessible because of the mesquites and thornberries. The bank was not as steep as I remembered, and the riverbed was dry and cracked. I stood there for a while, thinking about all of us who were connected to the river in some way. I looked downstream past the bend, and suddenly a vision of the Garden of Hearts stood clear in my mind. And just for a moment I thought I could hear Sam's voice. The wind does that. And sometimes, the *heart* does that. Finally, I started back.

I stopped as I entered the clearing and looked at Lorrie. She was standing now, leaning against the car reading her book. She wore jeans and a T-shirt from South Padre Island. It occurred to me that of all the places in this world she could be, it was her choice to be *here*. Waiting for *me*. My eyes filled with tears.

She glanced up and saw me watching her.

"Are you all right?" she asked.

I walked over to her. "Sure," I said.

"You don't look all right," she said.

"I'm fine. Really."

"Did you find what you were looking for?" she asked.

"I found *you*, didn't I?"

Lorrie smiled and kissed me. We hugged. After a moment, she started to let go, but I held on tight. I couldn't turn loose.

"I love you so much," I said. She squeezed even harder. Finally, we did pull apart. What little makeup she had on was streaked, her eyes shining.

"You dumped me for a cowboy," I said. "A danged ol' cowboy."

She smiled. "*You* gave up too easy."

"I told you we were meant for each other. That we belonged together."

"I thought you were weird."

"Now you know I was right."

She nodded. "Yes, you were. *Weird,* but right."

I paused. "Do you ever think about all the years we missed together?"

"Sometimes," she said softly.

"You were the prettiest thing I had ever seen."

She smiled big. "I still am."

We stood for a while holding each other. An eighteen-wheeler roared past and honked, raising a distant memory. Finally, I opened her door, and she climbed in. I walked around to the driver's side and stood for a moment. I'd never seen the sky so blue. Honest. Had it been on canvas, the painter would have used pure cobalt without adding any white or so much as a drop of linseed—and no artist is that brave. But with the whisper of its breeze, and the soft touch of an April sun, this day spoke of something more. Something extraordinary. *It seemed to beckon wonder.* And when I climbed in and closed the door behind me, that wonder came.

"Honey, the strangest thing happened while you were gone. This bird just flew down and landed on the fence post beside me and started singing really loudly."

I looked over at her.

"It was so weird. He just sat there and sang and sang. It was really beautiful. And then he took off and flew around right above me. Just back and forth. It was almost as if he knew I was watching him. Then suddenly he just flew away and was gone."

"What kind of bird was it?" I asked.

"I'm not sure. The sun was in my eyes, and I never got a good look at it."

I stared out my window.

"I really wish you'd been here."

"So do I," I said.

I started the car and pulled onto the highway. I tried to concentrate on the road. It wasn't easy. Several minutes passed before either of us spoke.

"What happened back there at the river?" she asked.

"Just now?"

"No," she said. "What happened in the past that made you want to come back?"

"A lot happened," I said. "A whole summer happened."

"Tell me about it. Tell me everything."

"I don't know, it's pretty long. It might take a while."

"That's all right. We've got time."

"It's a little sad in parts."

She paused. (Sad was not high on her list.) "Does it have a happy ending? Just as long as it has a happy ending."

I thought about that. I never had.

Does it have a happy ending?

I looked at this woman whose life I shared and felt so blessed to be a part of, and I remembered what Sam had said when I asked him about the River Big: *I reckon that's somethin' we each have to decide for ourselves*, he'd told me.

Then I knew. I reached out and took her hand. "Yes, baby," I said. "It does."

She smiled and squeezed my hand hard. Then she reclined her seat and turned to face me. "Okay," she said. "I'm ready."

I hesitated.

"I'm waiting," she said.

"First I have to tell you about that bird you saw back there," I said.

She looked puzzled. "What does that bird have to do with it?" she asked.

"A lot," I said. "Everything."

The time had come. I paused a moment longer, gathering my thoughts. Outside, I noticed the sun was plummeting from view. *This is some trail I'm about to lead her down,* I thought. *It's been such a long time, I wonder if I can still find my way.* Above us, the stars were racing to their respective positions. *I know the way. I'll always know the way.* The moon peeked over the horizon to be sure the sun was gone. Satisfied, it began its homeward journey. And as it did, we began mine.

"You've heard of Capistrano, haven't you?" I asked.

"Sure," she answered. "Why?"

I looked deep into her eyes. Then west, out my window, far into the remaining light.

"That was a swallow you saw back there," I said. "He's going home."

In my dream, I saw Rose and Sam sitting, hand in hand, on the bank of a big river. Tick the Dog was asleep at their feet, and nearby, children were playing. A man approached and introduced himself. He and Sam sat there and talked all afternoon. Mostly about baseball. And me. That man was my dad.

I awoke. I could feel Lorrie beside me, and Max at our feet. I wanted to wake them, and tell them, but didn't. It could wait until morning. I leaned over and softly kissed Lorrie on the cheek, then reached down and petted Max on his tummy. He was a little gray mutt with big black floppy ears and a single front tooth. Lost and alone when we found him. And unloved. But those days were gone. Here, love was abundant.

I closed my eyes and drifted back to sleep.

And all around us, the river flowed.

ACKNOWLEDGMENTS

My sincere thanks to:

Holly Porter, Angelia Thomason, and **Helen Thompson** for the time they spent proofreading, for their valuable suggestions, and for working cheap.

Gary Beesinger and **Charles Luig** for the liberties they allowed me to take with their lives for the telling of this story. I love you guys.

Laura Blake Peterson. Agents are the shepherds of writers' hopes and dreams. What an awesome responsibility that is. I am blessed to have her as the guardian of mine. YTB, Laura.

Jennifer Ehmann, my editor, for making mine a better story.

And finally, **my mom.** For everything.

On October 31, 2002, a stage adaptation of *River Season* was produced by Jerry Phillips at the Royal Theater in Archer City, Texas. The play, *There's a River Down in Texas*, was directed by Abby Abernathy. I owe a great debt to the entire cast and crew for their hard work and creative input, which was a huge help to me in completing the final revisions of the manuscript for this novel.

Cast and Crew

NARRATOR
Gary Beesinger

BEN
Chad Holland

SAM
Jim Black

PETE
Chance Gibbs

T. J.
John Cooper

ROSE
Tommye Wright

HARLEY
Craig Cowan

JOE
Jim Crowley

ALVIN
Greg Pollock

COOT
Jaron Curry

ROY
Clayton Clark

JESSE
Clyde Gardner

BILLY CONKLIN
Josh Howells

SHERIFF HARRIS
Bob Wright

DEPUTY DON
Mark Brown

YOUNG CLARE
Linda Lange

MARY
Jennifer Pool

CLARE
Barbara Phillips

ZACK
Luke Robinson

STAGE MANAGER
Tommye Wright

ASSISTANT STAGE MANAGER
LaRee Cowan

STAGE CREW
Clay Cowan
Brady Cowan
Jessica Carlisle

COSTUMES
Deanna Cowan

SOUND AND LIGHTING
Brandon Brown

VIDEO
Jerry Lee, Jr.

SET CONSTRUCTION
Brandon Brown
Jimmy Holland
Jerry Bradley

HOUSE MANAGERS
Suzan Eubanks
Christie Mooney

BOX OFFICE
Brandi Boren

ADVERTISING
Jenny Schroeder

·